YULE BE SORRY

PLANTED AND PLOWED
BOOK 3

LAINEY DAVIS

ABOUT THE BOOK

All I want for Christmas is my research back.

A herd of rogue goats ate my hydroponic fir trees and now their owner is working off the debt in my lab like a chaotic star of wonder.

Eliza Storm is everything I usually avoid—messy, unpredictable, and completely unimpressed by the precision of my greenhouse protocols. Worse, she thinks I'm a stuck up snob who's never gotten his hands dirty. Well, I think she's a reckless urban farmer with a demented donkey organizing her business.

When a winter storm traps us together in her barn, something shifts and I start to think I could fall for the woman who ruined my life.

But between my overbearing father using his influence to sway my investors and Eliza's scheming mother pushing her own holiday agenda, it feels like we're both stuck on the naughty list with no hope for holiday magic.

We don't make sense together anyway. She lives in a

nativity scene and my career is dangling by a piece of tinsel. Neither of us has time to cozy up by a yule log.

I'll just have to settle for a blue Christmas ... unless one of her goats has the power to guide this sleigh through the fog of red tape.

Yule Be Sorry is book three of the Planted and Plowed series of romantic comedies starring the Storm sisters. Love blooms reluctantly and stems get spliced in these steamy books full of small-town swoon in a big city setting.

STORM FAMILY TREE

EMMA STORM: MOTHER; NARCISSIST

ESTHER STORM: OWNER OF BRIDGES & BITTERS BAR, MARRIED TO KOA

EILA STORM: HORTICULTURALIST/HOPS FARMER, PARTNERS WITH BEN

EDEN STORM: BEEKEEPER, MARRIED TO NATE

ELIZA STORM: GOATHERD, SITUATIONSHIP WITH REED

EVA STORM: TO BE REVEALED…

AUTHOR'S NOTE

Look, I know what you're thinking. Hydroponic Christmas trees are probably not a viable business venture, and no reasonable person would force two strangers into an agricultural partnership over property damage.

You're absolutely right.

This book is holiday fluff of the most ridiculous variety, designed for pure escapist enjoyment during a season when we all need a little more joy and a lot less reality. So, please suspend your disbelief, embrace the absurdity, and let yourself get swept away by the magic of two stubborn people falling in love over tiny trees and unruly livestock.

Sometimes the most improbable stories make the best comfort reads.

1

ELIZA

I STARE AT THE EMAIL FROM BRAMBLEWOOD MANOR. They're willing to pay me five grand for a few days' munching from my wee herd of monsters.

Pittsburgh is overflowing with invasive vines, but I'm short on income as we sail into December. My Mobile Urban Natural Clearing Herd can be in and out of this fancy property in plenty of time for their Yule Gala, so this feels like a huge relief.

There are just a few small problems. Hiccups, really.

For starters, the city still hasn't paid me for my weed clearing work in Highland Park, and I'm caught in some endless loop of quarterly payment processing.

Which means I haven't been able to pay my hoof guy, so he won't sign off on my herd health, so... technically I can't say yes to this gig right now.

I write a quick response asking if they're at least able to pay half up front.

Then, of course, I need to ask Martinez if he'll accept

$2,500 toward what I owe him for just one more tiny little hoof check.

I sigh. I am so humbled by what I don't know about running a business. Nobody ever used the phrase "cash flow" in high school, and it's not like I had anyone showing me the ropes when I started up MUNCH. Heck, nobody even believed me that "goats as invasive weed control" is a viable business idea.

Well, I sure showed them. Sort of.

I gaze out the window at the pasture, where my sweet beasties are devouring another truckload of Timothy hay while their guard donkey, Chiron, looks on menacingly.

I'll never admit any of this, but these animals are truly naughty. Just a few months ago, they darn near wrecked my sister Eden's wedding by charging the couple just as they were about to kiss. Luckily, Eden and her now-husband were too lovesick to even notice something like a butt-butt from a goat.

It was just a gentle little tap, really.

My laptop pings, and I glance at the screen to see a response from Bramblewood.

> Dear Ms. Storm: We are delighted you are able to provide services as requested. It is not our policy to pre-pay. We can, however, offer a 10% deposit to retain your services if you could forward an invoice.
>
> Most sincerely,
> Mandy Warnick
> Event Coordinator

I blow out a long breath. I'm going to have to woman-up and make a stink with the city to get what I'm owed. What business can float five figures for an entire quarter? I really need to get better at reading the contracts I sign rather than just scribbling a half signature and hoping I'm not getting screwed.

This is why people hire lawyers.

I peel off my overalls and thermal and realize I'm wearing a super ratty sports bra and underpants I'd be ashamed to have a paramedic cut off me in an accident. I hear Chiron braying outside, yelling at me for being a perpetual slob.

Whatever. I spend the majority of my time with ungulates.

My clothes are functional. Except the sports bra. That's more of a *suggestion* of a boulder-holder at this point. I ransack my drawers, come up empty-handed. I can't go into a professional space with my boobs flopping around, small though they might be.

I decide to double up on the ratty bras and slide a dress over my head. Except the neckline of my cutest wrap dress reveals the fraying, gray top of the bras. I groan and rummage deeper into my closet, finding a cardigan with a hole in one armpit. *Real professional, Eliza.*

I ease my legs into some tights, which are in excellent shape because I never wear them.

Overall, I don't look too bad. I slip on some Maryjanes and jump in my truck to head down the hill and over the Allegheny River to downtown Pittsburgh.

It takes ages to find a parking spot, and it's nearly closing time when I finally make it through security and into the correct line. There's one person in front of me, a super tall dude in a dark pea coat. I spend a few minutes ogling the sharply creased navy trousers and smartly polished brown shoes he's got on. I can't see much else of him since he's leaned over with his hands on the counter, his dark head pressed against the glass, trying to shout at the clerk.

I get why they need these thick plexiglass dividers, but it sure makes it difficult to speak to the person on the other side.

Even so, this guy is more agitated than he ought to be. He hollers, "This is an agricultural product *and* a decorative item. They're *living trees*."

My ears perk up, and I can hear the tinny voice of the clerk. "Sir, your application says 'holiday decor.' That's category 47-B."

Mr. Tall and Well Dressed actually smacks the counter. "They photosynthesize. They have roots. Can you check with your supervisor about the proper category for nursery sales?"

I check my phone as he yells something about hydro-something not requiring soil and see I have just ten minutes before that irritated clerk puts a closed sign on her window.

She calmly tells him he only filled out a county form, and he needs a separate one for the city.

The guy tugs on his dark hair. "Is this not the city and county building? How can there be different forms? Can't you pass it down the counter to the right person?"

The clerk blinks at him. I grip my invoice. The guy yells something about an exemption for carbon-neutral initiatives, and I lose my patience.

"Oh, get over yourself. She said you filled out the

wrong form. Can *you* just grab a fresh one and let someone else have a turn?"

He whips his head around, glaring at me from behind a pair of thick frames. They're probably clear lenses he's wearing to appear smarter than he really is. I absolutely will not acknowledge that the look is working for him. I wave my hands like I'm shooing my goats.

He frowns. "You can wait your turn like everyone else, madam."

"*Madam*? That's rich. Look, you're not going to scold her into filing the form for you. These people are bananas about crossed t's and dotted i's. Ask me how I know." I rattle the invoice for emphasis.

He opens his mouth, but I elbow past him and smile at the clerk. "Hi." I squint to read her name tag. "Myrna. I'm Eliza Storm, here to check on the status of an invoice." I offer my sweetest smile—one my sisters tell me makes me look constipated because it's not genuine.

Myrna seems to agree with my sisters. Her facial expression is not encouraging as she peers at the invoice and slowly shakes her head. "Vendor distributions from the previous quarter are paid at the end of the current quarter. No exceptions."

My mouth drops and sweat pools at my lower back. This can't be right. I'm about to plead with Myrna for a partial payment when she grabs a CLOSED sign on a chain and hooks it over the microphone on her side of the glass.

I slap the window. "No, please, give me one more minute of your time."

Myrna shakes her head and is down a hallway before I can think of anything else to say.

Defeated, I turn to face the man, still standing there with his own form in his hand. I jab an index finger into his chest and sneer at him. "If you had just owned your mistake, I would have had more time to convince her to pay me, you pompous jerk."

His nostrils flare, and he applies downward pressure on my hand to remove it from his chest. A zing of sensation darts along my arm, but I'm sure it's due to heightened emotions.

"If you had gotten here earlier, you would have had more time to beg." He sniffs at me, turns on his fancy heel, and stomps toward the revolving door. Caught up in a flurry of frustration, rage, and despair, I follow him, not sure what I'm doing but certain I need someone to absorb all these big feelings.

"Hey, asshole!"

He doesn't turn, and I burst through the door to the crowded, rush-hour sidewalk and poke his shoulder. Okay, not his shoulder because I can't reach it. More like his spleen. He grunts and turns to face me. I wag a finger like some old nana. "Some of us work for a living. Don't you dare tell me to get here earlier. What were you doing all morning? Ironing your pants, or does your maid handle that?"

He stares at me for a long moment, his jaw working like he's chewing something bitter. Then, without another word, he turns and walks away, his expensive shoes clicking against the concrete with each deliberate step.

I stand there on the sidewalk, breathing hard, watching his back retreat until the city swallows him whole. My hands are still shaking—from rage or desperation or the lingering zing where our skin touched, I can't tell.

Same city. Same problems, apparently. Completely different worlds.

One thing's certain: this isn't over. Not by a long shot.

2

––––––––––

REED

The pH levels in my samples are off by point-zero-three, which may as well be a death sentence. I jab at the tablet screen, adjusting the solution for the third time today, my jaw clenched tight enough to crack molars.

"Easy there, Dr. Doom," my friend Paolo's voice echoes through the greenhouse lab as the bay doors slide open. "You're gonna give yourself an aneurysm."

I don't look up from the hydroponic data as Paolo makes his way through rows of my miniature fir trees sitting like tiny cub scouts, awaiting inspection. Each one represents months of research and more money than I care to calculate—money I don't have to spare.

"These stupid seedlings aren't cooperating," I mutter, making another adjustment on the dash. "Plus, I wasted an entire afternoon getting jerked around by some clerk downtown, so now I'm behind schedule. If they're not ready by next week—"

"Whoa, back up," Vick interrupts, appearing at my

shoulder with his usual unflappable calm. "What happened downtown?"

I look up to find all three of my friends standing in various states of post-work dishevelment—Paolo with grease under his fingernails from installing solar panels, Vick still wearing his city waste management polo, and Kash clutching a rolled set of architectural plans that probably contain his latest sustainable building design. It must be later than I thought if they're all here... which means I kept them waiting.

"Permit office," I say, the memory still making my blood pressure spike. "Tried to get my holiday tree classification updated so I'd have the right paperwork for the pitch event. Spent forty minutes explaining basic botany to a clerk who clearly hates her job."

"Ouch." Paolo winces. "Did you get it sorted?"

"No. Some woman started yelling at me for taking too long, and then the clerk closed her window." I turn to my seedlings, irritation flaring fresh. "Apparently, I was being 'argumentative' for asking logical questions about illogical categories."

I can't shake the image of that dark-haired woman jabbing her finger at me, all righteous fury and zero tolerance for bureaucratic nonsense. I keep wondering what had her so wound up. She struck me as someone who acts on instinct and deals with the consequences later, which honestly sounds... kind of liberating.

"Beer night," Kash announces, checking his watch. "You need it more than usual."

"I know, but—" I gesture helplessly at the seedlings that will make or break my entire future.

"No buts," Paolo says. "You've been in here since

dawn, probably haven't eaten anything, and now you're stress-spiraling. Plus, if you don't come, Kash is going to make us look at his drawings."

I open my mouth to argue, then realize I can't remember my last real meal. The past week has been a blur of analysis, growth projections, and increasingly desperate emails to potential financiers. The investor pitch-a-thon at Bramblewood Manor is my last shot at getting the funding I need to turn this whole Christmas tree thing from a crazy idea into an actual business.

"The pitch is in a week," I say, making one final adjustment to the grow lights. "If I can't demonstrate consistent growth patterns—"

"Then you'll have to charm them with your sparkling personality," Vick deadpans, earning snorts from the other two.

I shoot him a look. "Very helpful."

"Come on," Kash says, already heading toward the door. "We're going to Three Rivers Brewing. They've got that new IPA you wanted to try."

I hesitate, glancing back at my trees. They look healthy enough—vibrant green needles and strong root systems visible beneath the spongy soil alternative. Each tree is exactly eighteen inches tall, perfectly symmetrical, and completely sustainable. No soil depletion, minimal water usage, zero transportation emissions since they'll be grown locally.

My business targets young professionals who live in apartments or small condos but still want to decorate for the holidays. Enter: tabletop live evergreens. No need for a plastic tree and no sense driving to the countryside to chop down a full-sized one.

My idea is timely. It's environmentally responsible. It's trendy.

It's also bleeding me dry financially.

"Reed." Paolo's voice is gentler now. "They'll be fine for two hours. The robots will handle everything."

I know he's right. The entire setup is designed to run without supervision. But leaving feels like abandoning my post, especially with so much riding on next week's presentation.

"My parents called again," I say abruptly, staring at the trees.

The temperature in the greenhouse seems to drop several degrees. My friends met my parents exactly once, at my college graduation, and that was more than enough.

"What did they want this time?" Vick asks carefully. Vikram "Vick" Murthy is no stranger to rigid parents. We bonded immediately in the dorms once we realized we're both learning to let go of any hope of meeting our parents' expectations.

"The usual." I shake my head and release a groan. "Reminded me their 'offer' still stands—full funding for an MBA, fast-track into Nicholas Industries' executive training program, corner office by thirty..." I finally turn away from the seedlings. "All I have to do is abandon this 'hobby' and start acting like a 'responsible adult.'" My jaw tightens just thinking about my father's condescending tone.

"Fuck that," Paolo says with feeling. "This isn't a hobby. This is entrepreneurship."

"Try telling them that." I grab my jacket from the hook by the door, doing a final scan of the greenhouse.

Everything glows green on the status panel. "According to my father, sustainable agriculture is a luxury for people who don't understand real business."

"Your father's an ass," Kash says matter-of-factly.

Takashi, Paolo, Vick and I met freshman year and remained tight all through college and into grad school. I know I have zero interpersonal skills, but for some reason, the three of them put up with me and—I can admit this—drag me away when I forget to recharge my batteries.

We walk into the crisp November air, the industrial park around us mostly empty except for a few other startup employees burning the midnight oil. The Sustainable Innovation Incubator seemed like a dream come true when I got accepted here—affordable rent, like-minded entrepreneurs, access to shared resources. But the seed funding only lasts eighteen months, and I'm nearly through month seventeen.

"How bad is it?" Paolo asks as we climb into Vick's hybrid. "Financially, I mean."

I consider lying, but these guys have seen me through the initial excitement of developing the hydroponic method, the frustration of failed prototypes, and the crushing disappointment of my parents' reaction to my career choice.

"Bad," I admit. "I've got five weeks of operating expenses left. If the Bramblewood presentation doesn't pan out..."

I trail off, not wanting to voice the obvious conclusion. My friends exchange glances in the rearview mirror.

"We could—" Kash starts.

"No." I cut him off before he can finish the offer, my

words harsher than I intended. I see them exchange looks, so I take a breath. "I'm not taking money from friends. That's how relationships get destroyed."

"Stubborn ass," Vick says affectionately, pulling into the brewery's parking lot.

Three Rivers Brewing is packed with the usual Thursday night crowd—young professionals, a few students from local universities, and the hardcore craft beer enthusiasts like me, who can talk for hours about hop varieties and fermentation tanks. We manage to snag a high-top table near the windows overlooking the Allegheny River.

"Four pints of Eye of the Storm," Paolo tells the server, then grins at us. "I still can't believe it's made with locally grown hops."

I smile at that. My friends always support local business and share my opinion that it's important, not just stubbornly idealistic. The beer arrives quickly, and as expected, it's excellent. Citrusy and bright, with a complex flavor profile that speaks to quality ingredients.

Paolo reads aloud from the menu, telling us the hops are grown in reclaimed vacant lots, but the crop yield is only big enough for one small batch per year. "This is a rare, morally superior beer," he gushes, smacking his lips as we all agree.

"So," Kash says, raising his glass, "to proving that sustainable can be profitable."

"To not letting corporate assholes crush our dreams," Vick adds.

"To friendship," Paolo finishes simply.

We clink glasses, and for the first time in days, I feel some of the tension ease from my shoulders. Whatever happens with the Bramblewood presentation, at least I'm not facing it alone.

"Now," Vick says, setting down his beer, "tell us the truth. How confident are you about this pitch?"

I take a long sip, considering. "The science is solid. The environmental benefits are undeniable. The market research shows real demand for sustainable holiday traditions."

"But?" Kash prompts.

"I'm pitching to people who probably spent more on their last vacation than I've invested in my entire business." I stare into my beer, watching the bubbles rise to the surface. "What if they see me as some naive kid playing with plants?"

"Then they're idiots," Paolo says firmly. "And you'll find better investors."

I wish I shared his confidence. The truth is, I've already been turned down by other potential backers. The Bramblewood event is essentially my Hail Mary—a chance to present to multiple investors at once, alongside a dozen other amazing ideas from go-getters also seeking funding. This pitch event is for holiday-focused items, and there's an agreement we will leave our products in place as gifts for the estate's Yule Gala guests.

If it fails, I'll be back to square one. Or more accurately, back to my parents' corporate world, tail between my legs, and all my environmental principles neatly filed away as youthful folly.

My phone buzzes with a text from my mother:

Darling, don't forget about the Nutcracker tomorrow night. Your father has box seats.

I show the message to my friends, who groan in unison.

"The ballet?" Vick asks. "Seriously?"

"It's tradition," I say with resignation. "Nicholas family holiday obligations are non-negotiable."

"Skip it," Kash suggests. "What are they gonna do, shun you?"

The question hangs in the air longer than it should. Honestly, I'm not entirely sure they wouldn't. I don't *not* enjoy the ballet. I just don't have time to spare with so much riding on this pitch.

"Enough about my dysfunctional family," I say, raising my glass again. "Let's talk about something more cheerful. Like Paolo's latest solar installation disaster."

"Hey!" Paolo protests, but he's grinning. "That wasn't my fault. How was I supposed to know the client had a family of flying squirrels living in their attic?"

As my friends launch into their latest work stories, I relax for the first time in weeks. Maybe Vick's right; maybe the trees will be fine without my constant surveillance. Maybe the Bramblewood presentation will go well.

The server sweeps past in a flurry of dark hair that has me thinking about that woman who yelled at me downtown. Something about her fierce certainty... I bet she doesn't spend Thursday nights second-guessing herself over beer and fries.

3

ELIZA

"*You've got this, Liza.*" Eden's voice echoes in my head as I pull my rattling trailer up the circular drive of Bramblewood Manor, but her sisterly pep talk from this morning feels flimsy compared to the marble columns looming ahead of me.

The manor resembles a movie about rich people—all pristine white stone and perfectly trimmed hedges, with actual gargoyles perched on the corners judging everyone who dares approach. It's definitely weird to me that such an estate exists inside the city, but here we are. My rusty trailer bounces over cobblestones that probably cost more than my truck, and I can hear Chiron braying his disapproval from inside.

"Yeah, buddy," I mutter to my guard donkey, parking next to a gleaming catering van. "I don't like it, either."

The paperwork crinkles in my jacket pocket as I climb out. It's the hoof certification Martinez agreed to expedite after I promised him half payment by Monday and the rest... whenever I get paid. Which I will. Because I have to.

I'm adjusting my least-stained work shirt when a woman in a cream-colored suit clicks toward me on heels that could double as weapons. Her blonde hair doesn't even move in the November breeze.

"You must be the... animal service," she says, consulting her tablet with the enthusiasm of someone scheduling a root canal. "I'm Mandy Warnick, event director."

"Eliza Storm, owner of Mobile Urban Natural Clearing Herd." I offer my hand, which she eyes in disdain. "Ready to get your invasive plant problem sorted."

"Yes, well." Mandy's gaze darts to my trailer, where Chiron has started his *I-demand-attention* honking. "We have a very exclusive event coming up. Investors, innovators, Pittsburgh's finest entrepreneurs gathering, and then we have our annual Yule Gala." She pronounces it reverently. "The theme celebrates renewal and rebirth in nature, the return of light after darkness. Very symbolic."

I nod like I give a shit about symbolism. "Two events. Got it. Where's the work site?"

"Around back. I want to be very clear—you and your... livestock... are to remain completely out of sight during setup. Our presenters are displaying cutting-edge innovations in the main hall, and we cannot have any disruptions."

The way she says *livestock* makes my jaw clench. "My goats are professionals. They've cleared invasive plants for the city parks department."

Chiron emits a sound of agreement.

"I'm sure," Mandy says in a tone that suggests she's not sure at all. She winces as Chiron bellows again. I'd feel bad about the noise, but how else am I going to keep urban coyotes and other would-be thieves from my goats? Guard donkeys need to be obnoxious.

Mandy composes herself and continues. "Follow the service road. The affected area is behind the building." She waves a manicured hand as Chiron starts really yelling. You'll have access to water and electricity, but please keep noise to a minimum."

She clicks away before I can respond, leaving me with Chiron's commentary from the trailer. "Real charmer," I tell him as I climb in the truck.

The service road winds around manicured gardens that look like they've never seen a weed, past fountains and perfectly placed benches. Everything screams "we've got professional gardeners," right down to the perfectly uniform blades of grass all growing in the same direction.

I try to see it through my sister Eila's eyes. She's a horticulturist and would probably frown at all the pesticides it takes to keep the lawn this lush in late autumn.

I round the corner to the back of the property and find my kind of chaos.

It's at least half an acre of flora disaster. Invasive vines have claimed everything—knotweed strangling young trees, mustard garlic creating an impenetrable hedge, and enough poison ivy to hospitalize a small army. It's exactly the kind of ecological nightmare that gives me purpose.

I can see why Mandy Warnick hates it.

"Now we're talking," I say, parking next to a utility shed that's half-hidden under Virginia creeper.

I'm unloading fence posts when voices drift through

the open service door of the manor. Two guys in matching polo shirts lean against the doorframe, smoking cigarettes.

"...supposed to be some big presentation in the atrium," one of them says. "Revolutionary tree guy or something."

"Trees?" The other guy snorts. "What's revolutionary about trees?"

"Hell if I know. Rich people love weird shit. Remember that guy last year who had that poo-powered appliance line?"

"That was actually a pretty clever refrigeration system," the first guy corrects. "But yeah, trees seem like a stretch. Unless he's growing money on them."

"He grows them in water. Hydro something? Bah." They both stub out their cigarettes, heading back inside.

Hydroponic trees. I remember that uptight asshole from the permit office mentioning that exact phrase. Could that rigid dweeb be presenting at some fancy event *here*?

I shake my head and get back to work. Time to let my professionals loose.

Chiron practically explodes from the trailer when I open the back gate, immediately charging toward the thickest patch of mustard, offended by its very existence. The goats follow in a more organized fashion. Persephone and Ursula head straight for their preferred knotweed, while the younger ones start methodically working through the ground-level vegetation.

"That's my girls," I say, watching them settle into their work. This is what we do. This is what we're good at.

I continue setting up the temporary fencing, doing

mental math as I work. I estimate the goats can clear about a quarter of this space per day. Four days total, maybe three if they really get into it. The contract says I'll be paid on completion, which puts money in my account by Monday.

Finally.

I can pay Martinez, catch up on bills, and as soon as the city pays me, maybe even stock away a little for winter when work gets scarce. I realize we're just a few weeks away from Christmas, and nobody in Pittsburgh is thinking about their landscaping that late in December. I'm about to hit a major blank page in my work calendar.

Persephone bleats as she strips leaves from the vines she pulls down, and I grin. "Yeah, girl. We've got this."

A crash from inside the manor makes me look up, followed by someone shouting about proper handling. These fancy people really don't know how to relax.

I turn back to my work, already imagining the satisfaction of watching this tangled mess transform into an attractive landscape. When Pittsburgh's elite celebrate renewal and rebirth inside their marble halls, my goats and I will have delivered it.

I wonder what this *revolutionary* tree guy's innovation looks like compared to eight goats and a bad-tempered donkey. Probably involves a lot more paperwork and a lot less actual results.

But then again, rich people love complicated solutions to simple problems.

4

_____

REED

The trees look perfect. Absolutely perfect.

I step back from my display, checking everything one more time. Eighteen miniature fir trees arranged as charming centerpieces on tables, their needles a vibrant green that practically glows under the custom lighting Paolo and I spent two hours setting up.

"Dude, they're fine," Vick says from across the atrium, where he's adjusting a clump of twinkle lights for the third time. "Stop fussing."

"I'm not fussing. I'm optimizing." I make a minor adjustment to one of the trees, rotating it maybe two degrees. The look has to be flawless. Everything about this presentation has to scream professionalism, innovation, sustainability.

"You're definitely fussing," Kash adds, crouched behind the display table where he's threading extension cords. "The trees are gorgeous. The setup is gorgeous. You're going to kill this pitch."

Easy for him to say. Kash isn't the one who spent his

last dollar on fancy lights that make the trees appear lit from within. He's not the one whose entire future depends on convincing a room full of investors that hydroponic Christmas trees aren't just the next hot thing, but a lasting tradition about to arise.

Bramblewood's main atrium is honestly the perfect venue for this—soaring ceilings, natural light streaming through massive windows, and plenty of space for the forty-person crowd expected at the presentations. The whole Yule theme works in my favor, too. Renewal, rebirth, returning light after dark winter months. My trees embody all of that.

If I can just nail the delivery.

"Run through it one more time," Paolo suggests, settling into one of the chairs arranged neatly around the white tables. "Pretend I'm a skeptical investor who thinks trees are stupid."

"Trees aren't stupid," I say automatically.

"See? You're already defensive. Start over."

I clear my throat and straighten my shoulders, falling into presentation mode. "Good evening. My name is Reed Nicholas, founder of Urban Forest Solutions. What you see before you represents a paradigm shift in how we approach holiday traditions in an era of climate consciousness."

"Better." Vick nods. "Less robot, more passion."

"I was being passionate."

"You were reciting," Kash corrects. "Tell them why you care, not just what you're selling."

Right. Emotion. Connection. All the interpersonal skills that don't come naturally to me but apparently matter to investors who have money to throw around.

I try again. "Every December, millions of urban families drive to tree farms, cut down living trees, drag them into their homes for a few weeks, then throw them away. Meanwhile, apartment dwellers and environmentally conscious consumers either buy plastic alternatives that will outlive us all, or they skip the tradition entirely." I gesture to my display. "What if there was a third option?"

"Much better." Paolo grins. "Keep going."

"These trees are grown hydroponically in controlled environments using 90% less water than ye olde tree farm. No soil depletion, no pesticides, no transportation emissions. Each tree can be decorated, enjoyed, then placed on the windowsill until next year. They're living decorations that *improve* with age."

I'm hitting my stride now, the words flowing easier as I focus on the science rather than the marketability. "Urban Forest Solutions is perfect for apartment complexes, office buildings, and retail spaces to provide locally grown, sustainable holiday trees that—"

A crash echoes from somewhere behind the atrium, followed by ... bleating?

"Was that a goat?" Vick asks, looking toward the back of the building.

"Probably catering," I say, but something cold settles in my stomach. The sound is getting louder. And closer.

"Chiron, no!" a woman's voice shouts from the direction of what I assume are the service areas. "Get back here, you absolute—"

The door bursts open, and chaos floods into the pristine atrium.

A donkey—an actual, living donkey—charges through the doorway with the single-minded determination of a freight train. Behind him, a herd of goats streams into the space, their hooves skittering and sliding on the polished marble floors. They're bleating and scrambling for purchase, spreading out in a furry explosion across Bramblewood's elegant main hall.

And they're headed straight for my trees.

"No," I breathe, watching in slow-motion horror as wild ruminants bear down on months of research and my last hope for funding. "No no no no—"

A woman in dirt-stained overalls races after them, shouting commands the animals completely ignore. She slides across the marble in her work boots, arms windmilling for balance, and I realize with a jolt of disbelief...

I know that face.

It's her. The argumentative woman from the permit office who yelled at me for taking too long. The one who's been randomly popping into my thoughts since.

And she's about to destroy everything I've worked for.

"Stop!" I roar, lunging toward one of the tables just as the lead goat—a black and white spotted demon—reaches it first.

The goat looks at me with malicious satisfaction, then opens her mouth and takes a massive bite out of my tree. The one I spent fourteen weeks perfecting. The one that represents the ideal ratio of needle density to branch spacing.

"Persephone, *get down*!" the woman shouts, but it's too late.

The other goats have found my trees now, and they attack with the enthusiasm of creatures who've discovered a gourmet buffet. One knocks over my carefully positioned lights. Another manages to climb onto a table, its hooves scattering my informational pamphlets across the marble floor.

The donkey spots the backdrop banner and decides it looks delicious.

"Get them off!" I lunge for the spotted goat, but she evades me easily, taking half my prize tree with her. "Get your animals away from my trees."

"I'm *trying*." The woman dives for another goat, who promptly dodges her and starts working on the tree I've designated as my backup. "Ursula, I swear to god, if you don't—"

Two years of research. Two years of careful breeding, precise nutrient calculations, growth optimization. My entire life savings. My last chance to prove that sustainable innovation can compete in the real world.

Gone. Consumed by a herd of escaped goats while their owner slides around on marble floors in some kind of slapstick comedy routine.

"What the *hell* is *wrong* with you?" I explode. I don't even recognize myself right now, my usual composure cracking like an eggshell. "Can't you control your animals?"

Eliza whips around to face me, her cheeks flushed red with exertion and, confusingly, anger. "Can't you back off for two seconds while I handle this?"

"You call this handling?" I gesture wildly at the destruction around us. One of the younger goats has completely uprooted a tree and is now running in circles with it hanging from her mouth—a little green flag of victory.

"They got spooked. This isn't—" Eliza cuts herself off,

diving for the donkey, who's now shredding my banner with its yellowing teeth. "Chiron!"

My friends stand frozen at the edges of the chaos, Paolo's mouth hanging open and Vick already pulling out his phone to document what I'm sure he thinks is the most entertaining disaster he's ever witnessed.

But this isn't entertaining. This is my entire future being devoured by animals that should be nowhere near an innovation showcase.

This is the woman from the permit office destroying my life twice in one week.

As I watch the last of my perfect trees disappear into the mouth of a goat, I realize hard work means absolutely nothing when faced with pure, uncontrollable chaos.

5

———

ELIZA

I'M FUCKED. AND I FUCKED UP.

For some reason my goats listened to Mandy Warnick, clacking around in her spike heels.

At least long enough for me to usher them outside, where I'm now standing by the destroyed temporary fencing, awaiting my fate.

Reed Nicholas, the saintly dweeb who should not be this damn hot, slumps against the door panting, his dark hair sticking up at odd angles where he runs his hands through it every few seconds.

Reed is not wearing a suit or fancy pea coat. He apparently came to set up dinky trees in jeans and a flannel and damn if he doesn't grime up good. But I can't think about that right now.

My goats are now safely loaded in the trailer after twenty minutes of humiliating animal wrangling. I'm not entirely certain Reed isn't going to eat them.

Once I triple-check the trailer, I take a few deep

breaths and turn to face him. "I'm so sorry," I whisper. "I'm really not sure what happened."

He looks at me with wild eyes. "You're sorry?"

I nod. He nods. He swallows.

I knew the temporary fence had weak spots, but I don't have the capital to replace it. I fucked around, and now I'm going to find out the cost. The silence stretches until I want to climb out of my skin, broken only by the soft clicking of his stylus against the screen.

"Equipment damage," he mutters, obviously struggling to remain calm. "Custom grow lights, hydroponic systems, display materials..." More tapping. "Lost research time, replacement seedling costs, specialized nutrients..."

"Just give me a number," I say, my voice coming out rougher than intended.

Reed looks up, his eyes hard behind those thick glasses. "Not accounting for my time... fifteen thousand, one hundred and thirty-seven dollars. And forty-two cents."

The number hits me like a head butt from Ursula. I was expecting bad, but not this bad. Not "sell-my-truck-and-still-be-broke" bad.

"That's..." I swallow, my mouth suddenly dry. "That's very specific."

His nostrils flare, and his brows twitch. "I keep detailed records of everything." Reed's voice is clipped, professional. "Bear in mind, this represents approximately eight months of research and development. How would you like to handle payment?"

The question hangs in the air like a challenge. How

would I like to handle payment for thousands of dollars I don't have? "You don't have insurance or something?"

He takes another breath, twitches a bit, and squints. "Do *you* have liability insurance?"

This is very bad. I could ask my sisters for help, but Esther's already bankrolled me more than I deserve, Eila sinks all her spare cash into her hops farm, and Eden's still building her bee company. I could try to get a loan, but my credit history reads like a cautionary tale about what happens when you're self-employed and forget to make regular payments.

"I..." I start, then stop. There's no good way to say this. "I can't afford it."

Reed's jaw twitches. "Excuse me?"

"I can't pay that. Not right now." Heat creeps up my neck. "My business operates on really tight margins, and I haven't been paid for my last three city contracts because of some quarterly processing bullshit, and—"

"So you're saying you destroyed my work, and you can't make it right?" Reed's voice rises slightly, his composure cracking again.

"I'm saying I need time to—"

"Time?" Reed stands abruptly, flailing one arm in the direction of the goat-poop-smeared atrium. "The investor pitch is in a few days."

Chiron bleats from inside the trailer, traitorously agreeing with Reed.

I purse my lips and close my eyes, trying to think. This isn't like being evicted with a trash bag of school uniforms and second-hand shoes. I'm older now, and I have more resilience. "What can I do to make it right? Other than pay money..."

Reed's face vibrates, and I worry he's actually having a seizure. I wave an arm at the back lot. "I have a contract with Bramblewood. They're *going* to pay me. On Monday." I don't mention that they're not going to pay me *that* much, and most of what's coming in is earmarked for the farrier.

Reed wrinkles his nose and seems to come back into his body. "What do you have in mind?"

"You need to get more trees ready for the thingy, right? I'm really good with plants. Maybe I could work off the debt?"

"Absolutely not," Reed says immediately.

We're both so quiet I can hear the ticking of a watch. Is he actually wearing an old timey watch with hands on it? Of course he is. Meanwhile, I'm fifteen more thousand bones in the hole, and my business is in ruins.

I look at Reed, who's staring at me with an expression I can't quite read. Anger, definitely. But maybe something else underneath it.

Reed runs both hands through his hair. "Do you even know anything about hydroponics? You probably think nitrogen is laughing gas."

"Hey," I snap. "Don't assume for one minute I'm ignorant about nitrogen-rich soil. Just because I don't use fancy equipment doesn't mean—"

"This isn't about fancy equipment. This is about science." Reed gestures sharply. "You can't just throw some seeds in the dirt and hope for the best."

"I've been growing things since before you learned what chlorophyll was, pretty boy."

"Pretty boy?" Reed's eyebrows shoot up.

I stuff my hands in my pockets. "What's your alternative? You going to sue me? You've got limited time, right? I've got limited funds. But I'm good with plants. It's in my blood or something."

I swear he mutters something about bloody farm animals, but then he seems to melt into the wall of Bramblewood. I hear Mandy Warnick inside thanking the custodians for cleaning the atrium, her tinkling voice insisting they find some local artwork to hang while they wait for the replacement display trees.

"This is insane," Reed says finally.

"Tell me about it." I cross my arms and wonder how I ended up here.

"But," he says bluntly, "apparently this is the only way forward that doesn't involve court."

We size each other up for a long moment. He looks different than he did at the permit office—less stiff, more human. And, okay, he's really got the stern vibe that's got my insides churning. The tempest in the atrium cracked his perfect professional facade, and now I can see the stress underneath... the desperation.

"Right," I say, certainly recognizing that emotion. "But I have conditions."

"*You* have conditions?" Reed's voice climbs higher. "You destroyed my work, and you're making demands?"

I hold up a finger. "No talking down to me. I am not some ignorant farmer."

Reed's jaw works as if he's chewing on the words he wants to say. "And?"

"And no funny business at your place. I'm not in the market for bullshit harassment from lab assistants or maintenance guys."

"You actually think I have staff, who would—" Reed

stops himself, takes a breath. "Fine. Obviously, nobody will act inappropriately at the greenhouse."

"Good." I stand, suddenly exhausted by the whole disaster. "I need to get my goats situated, and then I'll head your way. Where's this laboratory of yours?"

Reed pulls out his phone and taps at it. "I'll send you the address." Reed nods stiffly. "Don't be late."

"Wouldn't dream of it."

"So let me get this straight," Eden says, passing me the bowl of pasta she made for family dinner. The five of us Storm sisters have always been tight, depending on one another when everyone else let us down, including our absentee mother. "You destroyed this guy's work, can't pay him back, and now you're gonna help him grow new trees?"

"That's the extremely simplified version, yes." I stab at my dinner with more force than necessary. "But it's not like I had a choice. Either I help tree boy, or I get sued."

"Tree boy?" Eila grins from across Esther's dining table. "Is he cute?"

"He's a pompous ass," I say quickly, trying not to think about how he looked in those glasses. Or why I'm interested in his buttoned-up mad scientist vibe. "Rich, entitled, probably never worked a real day in his life. You should have seen him robotically calculating damages down to the cent."

"Yikes." Eva winces. "That's cold."

"Right? And now I'm supposed to spend the next week learning his precious methods because apparently my twenty years of actual plant experience doesn't count for shit."

"Twenty years?" Eila's boyfriend Ben asks mildly. He's very literal.

"Fine, ten. The point is, this guy thinks technology is more important than good goat manure." I take an angry bite of pasta. "He probably waters his houseplants with a measuring cup."

"Okay, but Liza," Eden says carefully, "if you destroyed his work, isn't it fair that you help fix it?"

I glare at her. "Whose side are you on?"

"I'm on the side of you not going to jail," Eden shoots back. "This could have been so much worse."

"Could it?" I gesture wildly with my fork. "Now I'm stuck working with someone who thinks I'm some kind of hillbilly who doesn't know science from sheep dung."

"Do you know science from sheep dung?" Eila asks, grinning.

"I know enough," I snap. "I've been managing ecosystems while Mr. Fancy Pants was still trying to figure out which end of a plant goes in the ground."

Esther sets down her water glass with a sharp clink. "Eliza Storm, you are being ridiculous."

"I'm being realistic."

"You're being defensive," Esther corrects. "You messed up. This man is offering you a way to make it right instead of destroying your credit forever, and you're sitting here acting like he's the problem."

"He *is* a problem. People like him always are." I cross my arms. "Rich guys who think money and fancy equipment solve everything. He probably has no idea what real work looks like."

"You don't know that," Ben says quietly. Eila's boyfriend knows a thing or two about being misjudged. "Maybe give him a chance before you decide he's terrible."

"I gave him a chance at the permit office. He was a jerk then, too."

"Wait..." Eva straightens up. "This is the same guy from downtown? The one who was arguing about permits?"

"Yep. My luck is just that good."

"Okay, now it makes sense." Eden laughs. "You're embarrassed."

"I am not embarrassed."

"You totally are," Eila chimes in. "You had a bad day, took it out on some random guy, and now you have to work with him. That's mortifying."

"It's not mortifying, it's—" I stop myself before I admit... yes, it's absolutely mortifying. "Look, the point is I'm stuck. Ten days with someone who thinks I'm an idiot, doing work I apparently don't understand, all because my stupid animals got spooked."

"How did they get out, anyway?" Esther asks.

I shift uncomfortably. "Chiron found a rip in the temporary fencing and pushed on it. I knew it was loose, but I didn't want to spend money on new hardware when the old stuff still worked."

The table goes quiet for a moment.

"Oh, Liza," Eden says softly.

"Don't. I know it was stupid. I cut corners, and it bit me in the ass." I push pasta around my plate. "Story of my life. Pathetic."

"Hey..." Esther's voice is gentle now. "That's not true."

"Isn't it? I'm always scrambling, always behind on bills, always making do with equipment that's held together with duct tape and prayer. Now I've proven that my half-assed setup can destroy someone's life's work in about thirty seconds."

"Their life's work is pretty fragile if a few goats can wreck it," Eva points out.

Despite everything, I snort out a laugh. "That's what I said. Who designs trees that can't survive a little chaos?"

"Someone who's never met your goats." Eden grins.

"Exactly." I feel some of the tension ease from my shoulders. "Look, I'll do the work because I have to. But I'm not pretending this guy and I are going to be friends. We'll grow his precious trees, I'll finish my contract, and then I never have to see Reed Nicholas again."

"Reed Nicholas?" Ben's eyebrows go up. "As in Nicholas Industries?"

"How should I know?"

"That's a big company. Construction, development, energy stuff." Ben looks thoughtful. "His family has a hand in basically every project in the county right now."

"Great," I mutter. "He's not just rich; he's dynasty rich. That makes me feel so much better about this whole situation."

"At least you know he can afford to lose fifteen grand," Eila says cheerfully.

"Not helping."

Despite my grumbling, I feel a little better surrounded by my sisters' support. Even when they think I'm being unreasonable, they've got my back. And I'll need it.

6

REED

I PULL INTO ELIZA'S GRAVEL DRIVEWAY, MY HYBRID SEDAN jolting over potholes that could probably be classified as calderas. She never responded to my three texts about today's schedule, which means I have no choice but to manage this situation in person.

I'm also not entirely convinced she hasn't tried to leave town.

Her house appears held together by optimism and paint that might have been teal once upon a time. I'm surprised to see a number of different buildings—a real urban farm right in the middle of Pittsburgh's north side. Of course, Eliza has tools scattered across her porch haphazardly, along with mismatched watering vessels and roaming cats that probably have fleas.

But then I step out of my car and see the view.

Pittsburgh spreads out below me in the winter light, the downtown skyline crisp and gleaming in the sunrise. From up here, I can see the three rivers converging, the bridges spanning between neighborhoods like delicate steel vines. It's the kind of view that adds a few zeroes to a property's value, assuming anyone could navigate her driveway to appreciate it.

My gaze drifts to a large structure behind the house—some kind of barn or workshop that looks almost solid. With those south-facing windows and roof angle, it could easily be converted into a state-of-the-art growing facility. Climate controlled, properly ventilated, solar powered...

I'm mentally calculating square footage when an ungodly sound erupts from the building. I imagine an air horn mixed with a garbage disposal.

"What the hell are you doing here?" Eliza's voice carries from somewhere I can't see, tinged with surprise and irritation.

I blink and look around. "I couldn't get ahold of you and needed to confirm our start time for today."

A head pops up from behind a wooden fence, dark hair escaping from a messy bun and dirt streaked across one cheek, despite the early hour. "I said I'd be there."

"You didn't say when." I hold up my phone, displaying the unanswered messages. "I came to discuss logistics."

Eliza vaults over the fence with casual athleticism that makes me suddenly aware of my own physical limitations. She's wearing overalls again, these ones patched at the knee but clean, paired with work boots that have clearly seen actual work. It's alluring in a way that startles me. I... don't like women like this... usually.

"I was feeding animals," she says, wiping her hands on a rag. "Some of us don't check our phones every five minutes."

"I don't check every five minutes. I check at regular

intervals to maintain effective communication. And I've been reaching out since we left Bramblewood."

She stares at me until I have to check if I've just admitted to speaking fluent Elvish. "Right. Okay, professor."

I pull up my schedule on the tablet. "We need to establish a timeline for greenhouse shifts. The optimal growth window requires precise environmental controls, and I can't have you improvising when—"

"Hold up." Eliza raises a dirt-caked hand. "I need to finish feeding these guys and putting out fresh water or they're going to revolt. They should have been staying overnight at Bramblewood, but..."

She bites her lip in acknowledgement of yesterday's disaster.

"You're supposed to be helping me." I tap the screen. "According to my calculations, we need to maintain sixteen-hour photoperiods with specific wavelength adjustments every—"

An even louder bellow interrupts, this one definitely closer and significantly more threatening. Through the fence slats, I catch a glimpse of something large and gray moving with hostile intent.

"If you give me half an hour, we can get going." There's something mischievous in her expression. It makes me nervous.

I groan. "Fine. I'll meet you at the facility in..." I check my watch. "Forty minutes."

I'm halfway to my car when I hear hoofbeats behind me. I turn just in time to see a black and white goat charging directly toward me with the enthusiasm of a rabid golden retriever.

"She's just being friendly," Eliza calls, but her definition of friendly differs dramatically from mine.

I step sideways, tablet clutched protectively to my chest, trying to avoid the goat without actually running. My foot hits a patch of what I really hope is mud, and suddenly physics takes over.

The landing is significantly less dignified than I'd prefer.

I'm flat on my back staring at a gray November sky while a goat investigates my hair with aggressive curiosity. My tablet lies face-down in a puddle three feet away, and I can hear someone fighting a losing battle against laughter.

"Oh my god." Eliza appears in my field of vision, her hand pressed to her mouth. "Are you hurt?"

"My dignity has sustained irreparable damage," I mutter, not moving. "But physically, I appear to be intact."

That completely destroys her composure. She doubles over, laughter spilling out of her. "I'm sorry," she gasps between giggles. "I'm so sorry. It's just... I have this thing where I laugh when people fall, and I know it's not okay."

The goat chooses this moment to lick my cheek. "This is exactly why I work with plants." I sit up to assess the damage to my clothes. "Plants don't have vindictive personalities."

"Here." Eliza extends a hand to help me up, and I notice she's stopped laughing. "Cruella's actually the sweetest one. She was just curious about the stranger."

I accept Eliza's hand, surprised by the calloused strength of her grip. She pulls me upright with minimal effort, and suddenly we're standing much closer than necessary, her face turned toward mine with an expression I can't quite decode.

I gesture toward the goat. "You named her after a villain?"

Eliza tilts her head. "The villains weren't always evil." Something electric passes between us. Awareness maybe, or just the aftermath of shared ridiculousness.

"Your tablet," she breathes, but doesn't move to retrieve it.

"It's waterproof," I say, but don't move either.

We stand there for a moment, the morning air suddenly feeling warmer despite the chill, until another voice interrupts from the direction of the house.

"Eliza? Everything okay out here?"

A woman emerges from a van, and I immediately recognize the family resemblance—same dark hair, same direct gaze, though this sister moves with a different energy. More purposeful somehow. Gentle.

"Eden." Eliza jumps like she's been caught doing something inappropriate, which is ridiculous; we were just standing there. "What are you doing here so early?"

"Checking the hives before the weather changes," Eden says, but her attention is clearly focused on me. She takes in my mud-stained clothes and soaked tablet with obvious amusement. "You must be the tree scientist who's got my sister all beside herself."

Eliza's dark brows furrow. "This is Reed Saint Nicholas." She puts extra emphasis on the second word, which I don't understand.

"My middle name isn't Saint," I say, attempting to brush dried mud off my shirt with limited success, wondering what Eliza has said about me. Eden appears amused as Eliza releases an exasperated noise. I clear my throat. "And I won't be a tree scientist much longer unless your sister gets moving."

"He's very particular about schedules," Eliza says, and I genuinely can't tell if she's being sarcastic or appreciative.

Eden grins. "Perfect. Liza needs more structure in her life." She dodges the handful of mud Eliza throws at her. "Speaking of structure, you should come to our cookie exchange next Sunday. Very civilized, very scheduled. Right up your alley, Reed."

"I don't really do social gatherings," I say, which is true but sounds pathetic when said out loud.

"Neither does Eliza," Eden says. "You have that in common. Sunday at two, Esther's house. Liza will send you the address."

And then she's gone, disappearing around the side of the house like she didn't just meddle in her sister's personal life.

"She seems..." I struggle to find words.

"She's butting in," Eliza mutters, obvious affection in her voice. "You don't have to come. The Storm sisters can be overwhelming."

"It's fine," I hear myself saying, which is strange because I definitely meant to decline. "I like cookies."

Eliza stares at me for a moment, then shakes her head.

She nods at my tablet, now flashing with alarms for watering the plants. "Still works."

I begin explaining the wonders of waterproofing and realize something unexpected. The mud on my clothes doesn't bother me as much as it should. The chaos of this place—goats wandering freely, tools scattered, sisters coming and going—should trigger my anxiety.

Instead, watching Eliza listen intently to my explanation while Cruella chews on my shoelaces, I feel genuine curiosity about what comes next.

The realization overwhelms me to the point that I start sweating. I awkwardly snatch the tablet from Eliza and stomp my feet against the cold. "Well." I look up at the sky. "You said you need to feed your beasts something other than shoelaces." I wiggle my foot to dislodge the goat. "I'll see you at the lab."

I hurry into my car and get it turned around, but not before catching a glimpse of Eliza Storm's face, eyes dark with an indecipherable emotion.

7

ELIZA

My goats eat like they're half-starved while I replay Reed's abrupt visit. One minute we're having an actual conversation about water-resistant metals—which, okay, was kind of fascinating—and the next he's practically sprinting to his car like I threatened to brand him.

Men are weird. Rich men are weirder. And, unfortunately, hotter and harder to forget.

By eight, I've finished the animal chores and loaded a bag of my best composted goat manure into the truck. It's a peace offering... sort of. Eden's always going on about how goat manure is gardening gold. Lower nitrogen than chicken, perfect pH balance, breaks down slow and steady. If Reed's going to be all scientific about his trees, he'll probably appreciate quality organic matter.

I get the goats situated at Bramblewood and head north to Reed's evil lair, singing along to the holiday music on the radio. But only because I'm not hauling Chiron and I can hear things for once. I am not feeling festive. Absolutely never.

The drive to his place takes twenty minutes through neighborhoods that get progressively more corporate. Glass buildings, manicured parking lots, signs advertising "innovative solutions" and "sustainable futures." By the time I find the Sustainable Innovation Incubator, I'm feeling underdressed in my cleanest overalls and wondering if Reed's embarrassed to be working with someone who smells farm-fresh.

His greenhouse sits at the end of a row of identical units, distinguished only by a small placard reading *Urban Forest Solutions*.

I knock on the door, clutching my bag of manure to my chest.

Reed opens it, wearing a fresh button-down shirt and khakis that probably cost more than my monthly feed bill. He clearly showered after our muddy encounter, his hair damp and smelling of expensive shampoo instead of earth and animals.

"You came," he says, sounding surprised.

"Only to avoid court." I hold up the bag. "Brought you something."

His eyes drop to the canvas sack, and I watch his expression shift from curiosity to horror. "Is that...?"

"Goat shit. The good stuff." I push past him into the greenhouse, immediately overwhelmed by the sterile perfection of everything. It gives sci-fi movie vibes for sure. I clutch at the poo bag. "My sister Eila swears by it. Says it's better than any chemical fertilizer you can buy."

"Eliza." Reed's voice climbs higher. "This is a sterile environment. I can't have contaminants—"

"Contaminants?" I spin around to face him. "This is

premium organic matter. My goats eat the highest quality—"

"I'm sure they do." Reed holds up both hands in surrender. "But hydroponic systems use super precise nutrient solutions. Adding manure would throw off the entire pH balance, introduce unknown bacteria, contaminate the root systems—"

"So you're saying my shit isn't good enough for your fancy trees." Am I enjoying arguing with him about this? Everything is strange today.

Reed runs a hand through his still-damp hair. "I'm saying manure is an excellent fertilizer for traditional soil-based agriculture, but it's incompatible with my growing methods."

I set the bag down harder than necessary, irritation flaring. "Right. Because your way is better."

"It's not better; it's different." Reed's voice takes on that careful tone people use when they're trying not to offend. "Hydroponics eliminates soil-borne diseases, reduces water usage by ninety percent—"

"And costs a fortune to set up and maintain." I gesture around the greenhouse at all his fancy equipment. "What happens when the power goes out? When your computer crashes?"

"Those are manageable risks with proper planning and backup systems." Reed straightens, falling into lecture mode. "Traditional agriculture faces climate variability, soil depletion, pests, weather damage—"

"Traditional agriculture has been feeding people for thousands of years without anyone needing a PhD to grow a tomato."

"And look where that's gotten us." Reed's composure

cracks. "Topsoil erosion, groundwater depletion, pesticide resistance, climate change—"

"So, your solution is to grow everything in a lab?"

"My solution is to grow things more efficiently with less environmental impact."

We stare at each other across his robot workshop, the air humming with tension that's about more than farming methods. I can see the passion in his eyes, the genuine belief that his ideas will help save the world. It's... admirable, even if it's completely impractical.

"Fine," I say. "Explain it to me in words a simple farm girl can understand."

Reed's jaw tightens. "You're not simple."

The quiet certainty in his voice catches me off guard. "What?"

"You're not simple," he repeats, stepping closer. "You run your own business. You understand animal behavior... sort of." Reed moves closer, close enough that I can see gold flecks in his brown eyes. "And you pulled me out of a puddle with your bare hands."

Reed's looking at me in awe. "I was just trying to help."

"That's what I mean." His voice drops lower. "You don't think in terms of protocols or proper procedures. You just see what needs to happen and make it happen."

We're standing close enough I can feel the heat radiating from his body, can count the faint freckles across his nose. When did he get so close? When did I stop backing away?

"Reed," I start, but I'm not sure what I'm going to say.

His gaze drops to my mouth for just a second before

snapping back to my eyes. "We should... The trees need—"

A loud crash from outside breaks the moment. Through the tiny window in the door, I see one of Reed's neighbors wrestling with a dumpster. Reed steps back quickly, running his hand through his hair.

"Right," he says, voice carefully professional. "The trees. Let me show you the growing systems."

FOR THE NEXT HOUR, Reed walks me through his operation. He enthusiastically explains nutrient solutions and pH meters, light spectrums and growth cycles, speaking in the kind of technical detail that should put me to sleep but somehow doesn't.

Maybe it's the way his face lights up when he talks about sustainable agriculture. Maybe it's how his hands move when he's explaining something he cares about. Or maybe it's the way he keeps glancing at me to make sure I'm following along, like my understanding matters to him.

"So, the purple lights simulate the spring sun?" I ask, reaching to touch one of the tiny trees. Its needles are soft and perfectly formed, a fairy tale plant.

"Exactly. Blue light promotes vegetative growth; red light encourages flowering and fruiting. By controlling the spectrum, we can optimize each growth phase." Reed moves beside me, his shoulder brushing mine as he adjusts the seedling.

"And people will really buy miniature Christmas trees?"

"Urban consumers—city folks—want sustainable options that fit their busy lifestyles. Apartment dwellers, environmentally conscious families, people who don't want to drive to tree farms or deal with disposal..." Reed's hand covers mine on the pot, and I realize I've been absentmindedly stroking the tree's needles. "Plus, they stay alive after the holidays. Living decorations that grow year after year."

His thumb traces across my knuckles, probably without him even realizing he's doing it. But I realize it. I realize a whole lot about the warmth of his skin and the way his breathing has changed and how we're both pretending to look at the tree.

"Reed," I say again, and this time I know exactly what I want to say.

But his phone buzzes on the counter behind us, breaking the spell. Reed jerks his hand away as if he's been burned, immediately moving to check the message.

"It's Bramblewood," he says, scanning the screen. "They want to move the pitch-a-thon up to tomorrow."

"That's good, right?"

Reed's face pales. "If I have a product to show them, sure..." He stares at his seedlings despondently. "This is my last chance, Eliza. If this fails, I'll have to go back to my parents. Accept their money, their corporate job, their entire life plan."

The fear in his voice makes my chest tight. "I don't know what all that means, but that won't happen."

"You don't know that."

"I know you care more about these trees than anyone else possibly could." I step closer again, drawn by his vulnerability. "I know you're brilliant and passionate and too stubborn to give up."

Reed looks at me with an expression I can't quite read. "How do you do that?"

"Do what?"

"Make me believe things could work out?"

Before I can answer, his phone buzzes again. Reed glances at it with a grimace.

"My mother," he says. "Probably wondering why I missed the ballet."

"You should answer it."

"I should." But he doesn't move. "Eliza, about earlier, when I left so abruptly—"

"You got overwhelmed." I shrug, pretending it doesn't matter, even though it kind of does. "Happens to everyone."

"Not to me. I don't get overwhelmed. I plan for contingencies."

"Maybe you need more practice with chaos."

Reed's mouth quirks in what might be the beginning of a smile. "Is that what you are? Chaos?"

"Among other things."

His phone buzzes incessantly, and Reed sighs. "I should take this. Look around, but please touch nothing."

As Reed steps outside to take his call, I wander through his greenhouse, touching his trees and breathing in the fragrant air. Through the window, I watch him pace while he talks, his free hand gesticulating. I'm no stranger to uncomfortable calls with parents. I avoid my mother's calls more often than not.

He's nothing like the men I usually find attractive—too serious, too controlled, too concerned with doing everything perfectly. But there's something about the way he looks at his trees, the way he talks about sustainability and efficiency and making the world better.

And the way he looked at me when he said I wasn't simple.

My phone buzzes with a text from Eden.

> How's it going with tree boy?

I stare at the message, trying to figure out how to answer. I brought him manure that nearly gave him a heart attack. He talks about soil in a way that does things to my nether parts. Yet, he has the power to ruin me with one call to a lawyer. Everything is deeply confusing.

> Complicated

I bite my lip and add,

> Good

Eden responds immediately.

> The best ones always are.

8

—————

REED

THE GREENHOUSE HUMS WITH THE SOUND OF EQUIPMENT working overtime and my friends helping to bail my ass out. Paolo adjusts my backup grow lights while Vick measures nutrient solutions with the precision of someone who's watched me do it a hundred times. Kash crouches beside a tray of seedlings, documenting their progress on my tablet.

"These look good," he says, photographing a symmetrical specimen. "How many do you need for the presentation?"

"Twenty-four," I say, checking the time on my phone. Again. "Twelve for the main tables, twelve as backup in case of damage."

"How many are presentation-ready?" Paolo asks, smirking, though his tone suggests he already knows the answer.

I look around the lab, mentally cataloging each tray. "Sixteen. Maybe eighteen if I'm being optimistic about the ones still filling out."

"So, we need miracles," Vick says cheerfully. "Good thing you called in the cavalry."

The cavalry being these three guys, who showed up without question when I sent a desperate group text. They've been here since 6:00 pm, and it's now past eleven. Tomorrow is presentation day.

Eliza was here all day, distracting me more than she ought to, snapping at me for relying on machines she thinks are ruining everything, but she had to go tend to her villains.

My phone buzzes with yet another message from my mother about the "wonderful opportunity" to meet potential Nicholas Industries board members at tomorrow night's event. Apparently, half the city's business elite will be at Bramblewood's pitch fest, including my father's former business partner, who's now running a major development firm. I should feel happy that my parents are acknowledging tomorrow's event, but I know this is just lip-service enthusiasm. They really prefer I ditch the small business and join Dad's firm.

"Your parents again?" Kash asks, noting my grimace.

"My mother thinks tomorrow is my chance to 'network properly' instead of 'playing with plants.'" I set the phone facedown on the counter. "She's invited three separate investors to meet me, none of whom cares about sustainable agriculture."

"But they have money," Paolo points out.

"They have money *and* expectations. They'll want to see profit margins and expansion plans, not environmental impact studies." I adjust the timer on the nutrient pump, trying to channel my anxiety into useful tasks.

"My presentation is designed for people who care about sustainability."

"What about your dad?" Vick asks. "Will he be there?"

The question I've been avoiding. "Yeah. He always shows up to these things to 'maintain important relationships.'" I can hear the bitter edge creeping into my voice. "Should be fun explaining to him why I'm still playing scientist instead of accepting his job offer."

A sharp electrical pop echoes through the greenhouse, followed by the distinct smell of burning circuits. One of the main grow lights flickers, then goes dark.

"Shit," I breathe, rushing toward the affected section. A full quarter of my seedlings sits in sudden darkness.

"Can we fix it?" Paolo asks, already pulling out tools, twirling a hammer like he's a fancy bartender with a cocktail shaker.

I examine the control unit, my stomach sinking as I take in the melted wiring and fried circuits. "Not tonight. Maybe not at all." I groan and tug at my hair.

"What does that mean for the trees?" Kash asks.

I stare at the dark section, doing rapid calculations in my head. "Without proper light exposure, these seedlings will start declining within hours. By tomorrow afternoon..." I trail off, not wanting to voice the obvious conclusion.

"How many trees are we talking about?" Vick asks.

"Eight. Eight trees that I need for the Bramblewood tables." I run both hands through my hair, the familiar gesture providing no comfort. "Which means I'm going with an incomplete display and the joy of explaining to my parents why their investment in my education was wasted."

The three of them exchange glances, and I can practically see them trying to figure out how to fix something that can't be fixed with solar panels, waste management expertise, or architectural drawings.

"What about calling Eliza?" Paolo suggests. "Isn't she supposed to be helping you?"

"It's almost midnight," I protest. "And she doesn't know anything about grow lights."

"She knows about plants," Kash points out. "And emergency problem-solving."

I consider this. Eliza does have an annoying talent for seeing solutions I miss. But asking for help means admitting my high-tech systems are failing, that maybe there's truth to her criticisms about over-reliance on equipment.

Another glance at my darkened seedlings makes the decision for me.

ELIZA ANSWERS on the second ring, voice thick with sleep. "Reed? What's wrong?"

"I'm sorry to wake you. I have an emergency at the greenhouse, and I... you said you'd help with the trees, and I know it's late, but—"

"Slow down," she interrupts, and I can hear the rustling sounds of her getting out of bed. Oh god, I'm thinking about her in bed. "What happened?"

I squeeze my eyes shut to clear my head and explain about the light failure, the deadline, the eight seedlings sitting in darkness. She listens without interrupting, asking only a few technical questions about the lighting.

"I'll be there in twenty," she says.

"Eliza, you don't have to—"

"Reed. You called me, remember? I'm coming."

The line goes dead, leaving me staring at my phone while my friends pretend not to look smugly satisfied.

ELIZA ARRIVES WEARING jeans and a hoodie, her hair pulled in a messy ponytail. She is somehow more alluring than she was in the overalls. She nods at Paolo, Vick, and Kash like she's known them for years instead of having met them once.

"Show me," she says.

I lead her to the darkened section, explaining what each light array was supposed to accomplish. She crouches beside the seedlings, gently touching their needles and humming softly.

"The ones closer to the working lights are getting some spillover. But these four"—she points to the seedlings in complete darkness—"need help now."

"The replacement parts won't arrive until next week," I say. "Even if I could get them tomorrow, I don't have time to rewire the system before the presentation."

Eliza stands, dusting off her hands. "Who says we need the same system?"

"What do you mean?"

"You said the plants need specific light wavelengths, right? Blue for growth, red for flowering?" She's already walking toward my equipment storage, scanning the shelves with purpose. "What if we don't replace the fancy array? What if we just give them what they need to survive the next eighteen hours?"

I watch her pull out spare grow bulbs, extension cords, and clamp lights. "That's not going to provide the precise spectrum control—"

"But will it keep them alive?" she interrupts, connecting a red-spectrum bulb to a basic clamp fixture.

I consider this. "Probably. But the light distribution won't be even, and the intensity levels—"

"Reed." Eliza turns to face me, holding the improvised light. "Will it keep them alive until after your presentation?"

"Yes," I admit. "But—"

"Then that's what we do. Listen." She's already positioning the clamp light over the most vulnerable seedlings. "I once kept my sister's gecko alive for an entire winter after our electricity got shut off. I feel good about keeping mini trees growing." She tears a piece of electrical tape with her teeth, and I feel a sudden jolt in the crotch of my jeans. "We can fine-tune later."

As I watch her work, I stop worrying so much about the measurements and replicating these conditions. Instead, I stare at her long fingers and the way her worn jeans cling to her hips. What is wrong with me? Maybe I inhaled fertilizer gases or spent too much time with my hands near fir oils.

"Here," I say, grabbing another clamp light, desperate to regain some control. "Let me help."

For the next hour, we work side by side to create a makeshift lighting system. Eliza holds bulbs while I adjust heights. I calculate optimal distances while she secures clamps and runs extension cords. My friends help where they can, but mostly they stay out of our way as we develop a rhythm that feels almost natural.

"This one's getting too much heat," Eliza observes, touching the soil around a seedling. "Can we move the red light back a few inches?"

I measure the distance. "You're right. How did you notice without a gauge?"

Eliza shrugs and keeps poking around at my precious plants. I realize she's operating on instinct and some innate knowledge of agriculture, which is a little beside the point of what I'm doing, but somehow turns me on even more.

"This section needs more blue light," I add, noting the pale color of several seedlings. "They're starting to stretch."

Eliza repositions a bulb. "Better?"

I take readings with my light meter, amazed by how closely her instincts align with my protocols. "Perfect, actually."

By the time we finish, the improvised system looks like something a mad scientist would build in a disaster movie. Extension cords snake across the floor, clamp lights hang from every available surface, and the whole setup violates about twelve safety codes.

But it works.

"The seedlings should be stable now," I say, taking a final set of measurements.

"And tomorrow's presentation?" Eliza asks.

I meet her gaze and swallow, staring into her brown eyes as she seems genuinely concerned with my work. "Should go fine. Assuming I don't completely humiliate myself in front of my father and half of Pittsburgh's business community." I realize how that sounds and quickly add, "Not that I'm nervous or anything."

Eliza gives me a look that suggests she's not buying my casual tone. "Your dad's going to be there?"

"Unfortunately. Along with several of his company's board members and what my mother describes as 'serious investors who understand *real* business.'" I can't keep the bitterness out of my voice. "Should be fun... explaining sustainable agriculture to people who think environmentalism is a hobby for trust fund kids."

"Is that what they think you are?" she asks. "A trust fund kid playing with plants?"

The question hits harder than it should. "Sometimes I wonder if they're right." We stare at one another for a few beats before I sigh in resignation. "Anyway, thank you. For coming. For helping."

"My pleasure." She grins. "Though next time, maybe don't wait until everything's falling apart."

"Noted." I glance around the greenhouse, taking in the chaos of equipment and extension cords. I realize my friends have curled up on a pile of cardboard in the corner, sleeping. "I should clean this and head home. Tomorrow's going to be..."

"Brutal," she finishes. "But you'll be amazing. Your trees are perfect, your presentation is solid, and anyone who doesn't see the value in what you're doing is an idiot."

I want to believe her confidence in me is justified, and I'm a little taken aback by her pleasant attitude. Maybe she's friendlier when she's tired. "Will you... would you consider coming tomorrow—today, I guess? To the presentation?"

Eliza's eyebrows shoot up. "Me? At a fancy investor thing?"

"It's not that fancy. Well, it is, but…" I fumble for words, not entirely sure why I want her there. "You understand the trees, and I think I present better when I'm not just talking to spreadsheet people."

"I don't exactly fit in with the yacht club crowd."

"Good," I say firmly. "Maybe they need someone who doesn't fit."

She studies my face for a moment, then nods slowly. "Okay, but I'm not wearing a dress."

"I wouldn't expect you to."

I nudge my friends awake, and they blink at me, wave a hand, and roll over. I guess they're staying the night. Eliza yawns and heads toward the door, so I trot after her, wanting to make sure she gets to her truck okay. Should it be this… titillating when a woman drives a pickup truck?

Something compels me to stand nearby, watching with my hands in my pockets as she waves, climbs into the driver's seat, turns the key in the engine and …

"Is it supposed to sound that way?" I step closer to the groaning vehicle as Eliza smacks the steering wheel with a curse. "When's the last time you had it serviced?"

"Serviced?" Eliza laughs, but it sounds forced. "Reed, I change the oil and pray to whatever elves tend rusty vehicles. That's about the extent of my maintenance budget."

The truck gives a final whine, and then there's nothing but a clicking sound when she turns the key. "Shit," she mutters, trying again with the same result.

"I'll drive you home," I offer.

"You don't have to—"

"Eliza. It's two-thirty in the morning, and your truck just died in an industrial park. I'm driving you home."

She looks like she wants to argue, but practicality wins out. "Fine."

The drive to her place is quieter than I expected. Eliza stares out the passenger window as we enter the city, the lights of the downtown skyscrapers illuminated for the holiday season. Each of the bridges seems to have a different theme, from Hanukkah blue and silver to a Kwanzaa kinara, and Eliza is noticeably charmed by all of it.

I find myself stealing glances at her profile in the dashboard light. She looks tired but alert, clearly processing the events of the evening.

I navigate the narrow streets of her neighborhood, noting the mix of renovated houses and ones that have seen better days. Eliza's place sits on a hill with that spectacular view of the city, and she sighs, gazing at the glittering lights.

"Thanks for the ride," she says when I pull over. "And for letting me help tonight. It was kind of fun, solving problems with duct tape."

"Thank you for making it work," I reply. "I was feeling pretty forlorn about the whole thing."

She grins. "Sometimes good enough is better than perfect."

"Don't let that get around. My reputation as a control freak is all I have left."

Eliza laughs, then grows serious. "You're going to do great tomorrow, Reed. Trust your instincts."

She gets out of the car and walks toward her house, fumbling for keys in the darkness. I should leave now; she's safely home, my obligation as a decent human being is fulfilled. But I find myself sitting in the driveway, engine running, watching until she gets her front door open and disappears inside.

A light comes on in what I assume is her kitchen, then another in an upstairs window. Only then do I put the car in reverse and head home.

The whole drive to my apartment, I can't shake the image of Eliza working beside me in the greenhouse, completely focused and utterly competent. She never once questioned whether we could fix the problem. She just started fixing it.

Later today, I'll present my trees to a room full of investors and family members who may or may not understand what I'm trying to accomplish. But tonight, for the first time in months, I believe the presentation might succeed.

And it's not just because of the trees.

9

____

ELIZA

REED CALLS WHILE I'M MUCKING OUT THE GOAT SHELTER, which means I answer with my phone tucked between my shoulder and ear while scraping questionable substances off concrete.

"I know you're probably busy," he says without preamble, "but would you let me buy you lunch? As a thank you for last night."

I pause mid-scrape. "You don't owe me lunch for helping with your lights."

"Maybe not, but I could use a pep talk before tonight's presentation." His voice carries that tight edge I'm starting to recognize as Reed trying not to sound anxious. "And I was thinking we could go to the Christmas market downtown. I know some vendors there, and after seeing what your goats do to regular plants, I believe in them when it comes to weeds on my friends' properties."

"You want to pimp out my goats at a Christmas market?"

"I want to introduce you to people who need your

services," he corrects. "There's a guy who's converting old warehouses into artist studios. Another woman who's rehabbing industrial buildings for small manufacturers. The kind of properties that have been sitting empty long enough for invasive vines to take over... Anyway, they have booths there if you want to meet them."

I lean against my pitchfork, considering. The city still hasn't paid me for the Highland Park job, and winter work is always scarce. Plus, Reed sounds nervous about tonight, which is weirdly endearing coming from someone who usually has everything calculated to three decimal places.

"What time?" I ask.

"Two? I know it's late for lunch, but—"

"Two works. Where should I meet you?"

"Downtown. By the ice rink?"

After we hang up, I stare at my reflection in the barn window. If Reed's introducing me to potential clients, I should probably look professional and businesslike instead of resembling someone who's been wrestling goats all morning.

Thankfully, the truck just needed a jump and a new battery, but I'm already dancing on a haystack when it comes to my budget. I decide I'll accept Reed's free lunch.

I hope he wears his glasses again.

AN HOUR LATER, I'm standing in front of my closet in an actual panic. Everything I own falls into two categories: farm work clothes and the single dress I wear to weddings... or downtown when I plead with the city to pay me. Neither seems appropriate for lunch before a business presentation. I am obviously primarily concerned with the impression I'll make on potential clients and absolutely not the nerdy tree scientist who smells pine fresh. He would be a distraction, and I'm way too broke to let myself get distracted.

Eventually, I settle on my best dark slacks and a bright blue sweater Eden bought me last birthday. I've never worn it because it seemed too nice for everyday. I even dig out a scarf—a soft gray one Esther gave me years ago that still has the tags on it. It's like my sisters are trying to send me messages through cozy fabric.

By the time I reach downtown, the sun is already slanting low between the buildings, casting everything in that golden light that makes Pittsburgh look like a postcard. It gets dark so early this close to the solstice, but I don't mind as I look at the scene before me. The Christmas market spreads across the plaza in front of PPG Place, wooden booths arranged in neat rows near the ice rink, where the city installed a massive Christmas tree my goats would devour in a heartbeat.

I spot Reed immediately, standing near the rink entrance in his dark wool coat. And the glasses. Damn him for looking vulnerable *and* smart *and* mysterious. When he turns and sees me, his face lights up in a way that makes my stomach do something acrobatic. I need to remember this man holds the power to ruin me.

"You look..." He stops, seeming to search for words as his gaze travels from my face down to my boots and back up. "Really nice. Different. Good different."

"Thanks." I feel heat creep through my neck despite the cold air. "You clean up pretty well yourself."

His dark hair is doing that thing where it's perfectly messy, like he ran his hands through it but somehow made it look intentional. And he smells like those beautiful fir trees he's always coddling. I definitely don't hate it.

"Come on." He offers me his arm. "Let me show you around."

The market feels totally different when I'm here with a guy. Not that this is a guy-guy. Reed Saint Nicholas is the supervisor of my restitution for naughty goat behavior. That's it.

But as Christmas music drifts from speakers hidden among the booths, mixing with the sound of a flute band performing near the tree, it's easy to forget this isn't a date. Skaters glide around the rink, their laughter echoing off the surrounding glass buildings. The air smells of cinnamon and roasted nuts and that crisp winter scent that makes everything feel like a storybook.

"This is incredible," I say, stopping to watch a glassblower shape ornaments at his booth. The molten glass glows orange in his hands, transforming into delicate spirals and flowers as we watch.

"Pittsburgh does holiday magic right." Reed guides me toward a booth selling handcrafted jewelry. "The guy I mentioned is somewhere with the metalworkers."

We wander through the rows, Reed smiling at children and couples. A woodworker carves intricate nativity scenes. A woman sells hand-knitted scarves in every color imaginable. A couple offers chocolate truffles shaped like tiny presents.

"Reed!" a voice calls from behind us.

We turn to see an Asian woman about my age

approaching, her magenta hair escaping from a knitted hat. She's wearing work boots and paint-stained jeans under a thick coat, but somehow manages to look effortlessly put together.

"Maya," Reed says, his face brightening. "I was hoping I'd run into you. Maya Chang, meet Eliza Storm. Eliza, Maya owns Riverside Studios."

Maya extends a hand that's strong and paint-stained. "Nice to meet you. Reed's told me about your goat business."

"He has?" I glance at Reed, surprised.

"I was telling Maya about what you did at Bramblewood," Reed explains. "She's been dealing with invasive vines at her warehouse complex for months."

"Poison ivy," Maya says with feeling. "English ivy. Some kind of vine that might actually be strangling the building. I've had three landscaping companies tell me they can't handle it unless they use so many chemicals I'd have to evacuate the artists."

"Goats love English ivy," I say automatically. "And poison ivy doesn't bother them at all. How many acres are we talking about?"

As Maya describes her property, I find myself getting excited. It's exactly the kind of work my herd excels at, and they could clear her property in a matter of days if it doesn't snow. We exchange contact information, Maya promising to call next week to schedule a site visit.

"That was amazing," Reed says after Maya heads to her booth. "You should see your face when you talk about your work."

"What do you mean?"

"You light up. Like you're talking about something you love instead of just a job."

Before I can respond, he's steering me toward a booth selling roasted nuts. The vendor recognizes Reed immediately, calling out a greeting in Italian.

"Due coni, per favore," Reed says, holding up two fingers.

The man grins and fills two paper cones with hot almonds, the steam rising in little clouds between us. Reed hands me one, his fingers brushing mine as I take it.

"You speak Italian?" I ask, warming my hands on the cone.

"A little. My grandmother on my mother's side. She used to make these nuts every Christmas." Reed's voice gets softer. "It's one of the few family traditions I miss."

We find an empty bench facing the ice rink, close enough to hear the scrape of skates on ice and the cheerful chaos of families learning to skate together. I bite into the warm nuts, savoring the sweet, nutty flavor. "How do you know all the market vendors?"

Reed chews thoughtfully. "I met a lot of them in the startup cohort for my tree business." Reed waves a hand at the wooden booths. "I had hoped to be up and running this year, but things got delayed. So, I drowned my sorrows in spiced cider..."

He laughs and shakes his head, popping a handful of nuts into his mouth. "I like being here more than being with my family this time of year."

I laugh, but it's not bitter. "The Storm sisters' approach to Christmas was... creative. One year we had no money for presents, so we made coupons for each other. Good for one free hair braiding, one batch of cookies, one night of doing someone else's chores. That sort of thing."

"That sounds nice."

"It was." I'm surprised to realize I mean it. "Better than the years Mom was around and tried to make everything 'perfect' only to ditch us for happy hour with her favorite barflies. Esther always said the best Christmases were the ones when we just had each other."

Reed is quiet for a moment, watching a little girl in a pink coat wobble across the ice while her father skates backward in front of her, arms outstretched.

"We had these elaborate Christmas Eve dinners," he says. "Catered affairs with the right China and the right wines and conversation topics approved by my mother. I used to time how long we could go without anyone mentioning business or stock prices or who was donating what to which charity."

"What was your record?"

"Twelve minutes." Reed grins, but there's sadness in it. "Usually broken when my father started lecturing me about my 'phase' and when I was going to grow up and join the real world."

I want to reach over and touch his hand, but I don't quite dare. Instead, I shake more cinnamon nuts into my mouth. "For what it's worth, I think what you're doing is pretty real."

"Even if it's too dependent on technology?"

"Even if you sometimes need extension cords and duct tape to make it work."

That gets a real smile out of him.

We spend a damn-near perfect afternoon wandering around, munching and taking in the sights. Around us, the market glows as vendors switch on their string lights. The sun has disappeared behind the buildings, leaving the sky that deep blue color that only appears in winter. The Christmas tree lights reflect off the ice, creating patterns that shift and dance with each passing skater.

"We should probably head to Bramblewood soon," Reed says, but he doesn't move. "I need to set up for the presentation."

"Nervous?"

"Terrified," he admits. "What if they hate it? What if my father was right, and this whole thing is just an expensive hobby?"

I study his profile in the twinkling lights, the way his jaw tightens when he's worried, the way his glasses catch the reflection of the Christmas tree. "Reed, look at me."

He turns, and I'm struck again by how his eyes look almost golden in this light.

"You're going to be brilliant," I say firmly. "You believe in what you're doing, and anyone who doesn't see that is missing out on something extraordinary."

Reed stares at me for a long moment, and I feel the electric awareness that's been building between us for days. The space between us seems to shrink, and I think he might lean closer, might finally—

"Excuse me," a voice interrupts. "Are you folks ready to move along?" We look up to see a security guard smiling apologetically. "We're starting to close the ice rink for the evening. Private event."

"Of course." Reed stands quickly. "Sorry."

As we gather our things, Reed pauses at a booth selling handcrafted ornaments. The woman behind the counter has dozens of tiny animals carved from wood—foxes, rabbits, owls.

And goats.

"How much for this one?" Reed asks, picking up a small wooden goat with tiny horns and an expression that somehow manages to look both mischievous and dignified. Reed hands over his credit card before I can protest. "For your tree," he says, offering me the ornament. "If Cruella doesn't eat it first."

I take the little goat, running my thumb over the smooth wood. It's perfectly carved, every detail precise but somehow full of personality. It does indeed look like my girl.

"Thank you," I say, and mean it. "I love it."

As we walk toward where we parked, Reed's scarf comes loose in the wind. Without thinking, I reach up to fix it, my fingers brushing his neck as I tuck the soft wool back into his coat.

"There," I say, suddenly aware of how close we're standing, how my hands are still resting on his coat collar.

Reed's eyes drop to my mouth, then back to my eyes. "Eliza..."

"Yes?"

But whatever he was going to say gets lost as a group of laughing teenagers pushes past us, breaking the moment. Reed runs that familiar hand through his hair.

"We really should get going," he says.

As we walk through the glittering downtown streets, I clutch the wooden goat in my pocket and try to process what just happened. Reed is not the uptight rich boy I thought he was. He's passionate and vulnerable and, apparently, thinks I'm extraordinary.

10

REED

THE ATRIUM AT BRAMBLEWOOD MANOR GLOWS WITH holiday warmth and startup anxiety. My trees—all twenty-four we coaxed through despite the odds—serve as centerpieces on the tables, with the extras decorating the buffet. Their wee needles seem to wave under the twinkle lights Eliza helped me rig after our hot nut lunch.

It wasn't a date, and that's because I'm in a position of power over her regarding this very estate, and I would do well to remember that.

I adjust my tie for the tenth time, running through my presentation notes. The room is filling with the investors I need: men in expensive suits, women in jewelry that costs more than my hybrid sedan, and nonbinary super-stars with exquisite socks—Pittsburgh's angel investors gathering to see which businesses will get their wings.

I wish I wasn't staring at my parents at one of the tables.

My mother catches my eye, and her smile feels bright

and artificial. My father sits beside her with his face in his phone. I know they sought invitations, always butting in.

"Reed." Mandy Warnick appears at my elbow, consulting her tablet. "We're ready to begin whenever you are."

I nod, scanning the crowd for Eliza. She said she'd be here after she checked on the herd, but I don't see her anywhere among the designer dresses and perfectly styled hair.

Then a side door opens, and there she is.

She ditched her coat somewhere and looks stunning in a blue sweater, her eyes impossibly dark. Her hair is pulled in a simple ponytail, and she seems right at home among this crowd, even though she said she hates wealthy people. Eliza finds a seat at a table near the back and smiles at me above the polished heads.

I have eyes only for her as I approach the podium, my nerves slipping into an emotion-cocktail of sexual frustration, attraction, and financial terror.

"Welcome, everyone," Mandy announces. "We are so excited to begin our showcase this evening. We've got some incredible budding businesses growing right here in Pittsburgh, and I know you're all eager to learn about them. Up first, we have Reed Nicholas of Urban Forest Solutions."

I smile through the polite applause, keeping my gaze locked on Eliza and hoping this gives me an air of studying the entire audience. She is calm and still, her blue sweater reminding me of the evening sky. She's a friendly face in a room full of vultures who might determine my entire future.

I guess it's wrong to think of investors as carrion birds, but it's hard not to feel a bit like roadkill, especially since my first and most perfect batch of trees was eaten by goats in a matter of minutes.

"Good evening," I begin, my voice steadier than I feel. "Each of your tables features my flagship product." I pause while people look and nod at their centerpieces. "These aren't just mini Christmas trees. They represent a fundamental shift in how we think about urban agriculture and sustainable holiday traditions."

I fall into my rhythm, explaining the hydroponic system, the environmental benefits, the market potential. Every time I start to feel overwhelmed by the magnitude of what I'm proposing, I look at Eliza. She's leaning forward slightly, focused entirely on what I'm saying, and somehow that makes everything else fade into the background.

I warm up a bit and talk about pesticides, the ways I avoid them, and the benefits of living decorations people can admire year-round.

A hand shoots up in the audience. "What's your projected return on investment?" asks a man I recognize as one of my father's golf partners.

"Based on market research and pre-orders already secured, we're projecting thirty percent growth year over year for the first five years," I respond, grateful for all the hours I spent perfecting these numbers.

More questions follow. Production costs. Scalability. Distribution logistics. I answer each one with confidence, occasionally glancing at my notes but mostly speaking from months of preparation and genuine passion for the project.

I'm explaining the potential for expansion into other plant products when I hear it—the distinctive sound of my father's laugh. Not amused laughter, but the condescending chuckle he reserves for ideas he finds naïve.

"Well," Mandy Warnick's voice tinkles from the audience, "I think we've all heard enough to get the picture."

She approaches the podium, perfectly coiffed, with an iron-on smile. I nod and back away as she introduces the next presenter. Taking my seat at a side table, I try to listen politely to presentations about bespoke shirts and mineral deodorant. Then I try to tune out and silence the inner critic insisting these presentations are all superior to mine.

When it's over, my father stands up and the entire room seems to shift its attention to him. Charles Nicholas commands attention wherever he goes, a skill honed by decades of closing million-dollar deals and intimidating anyone who dares challenge his authority.

"I have to say, son, this is quite an impressive... hobby you've developed here." He strides toward me, waving to his acquaintances. "Very academic."

The word drips with disdain, and I feel my dreams crumbling around me.

"But I think what our investors here are interested in," my father continues, clapping me on the back hard enough to make me stumble slightly, "is a real business opportunity. Scalable ventures with proven market demand."

"This is a proven concept," I say, trying to maintain my professional composure while my father effectively dismantles everything I've worked for. I can already feel the crowd drifting toward the deodorant people. "The environmental benefits alone—"

"Oh, the environment." My father waves a dismissive hand. "Of course, of course. Very important for the young generation to feel good about their purchases. But at the end of the day, Nicholas Industries understands that business is about profit margins, not saving the world."

The room has gone completely silent. I can feel dozens of eyes watching this public humiliation, and I'm powerless to stop it without creating an even bigger scene.

"As a matter of fact," my father continues, his voice carrying to every corner of the atrium, "Reed will be joining the family enterprise in the new year. We're launching a sustainable development division, and this little tree experiment will make an excellent pilot project. Under proper supervision, of course."

My mouth goes dry. "Dad, that's not—"

"I know you'll all want to discuss the investment opportunities this presents," he bulldozes over my protest. "Ah, and who is this?"

He gestures to my side, where Eliza stands holding my tablet, her nose wrinkled in disdain she doesn't bother to hide.

"Eliza Storm," she says, her voice thick with scorn. "I need to borrow Reed for a minute—"

"You must be his assistant." My father plows forward like a combine harvester, slicing away my dignity along with my plans. "Been helping our Reed with his little project, dear?"

Every head nearby turns to look at Eliza, and I watch her face transform. The calm confidence disappears entirely, replaced by something cold and distant. Her eyes meet mine, and I sense her waiting for me to lead what happens next.

I should correct him. Should announce that Eliza is a business owner in her own right. My friend, not my employee. I should tell this room full of potential investors she's the reason these trees survived long enough to be presented at all.

But my father's hand is still on my shoulder, his presence overwhelming, and the words stick in my throat like they always do when he's asserting his authority.

"Thank you all for coming to hear my boy," my father says to his rich friends, as if this were his event to conclude. "We'll be in touch with detailed prospectuses for those interested in serious investment."

The crowd disperses, heading in earnest toward the bespoke clothing guys. Several people approach my father, shaking his hand and discussing indoor tennis at the club.

I stand frozen, watching Eliza gather her coat from the back of her chair. She moves with deliberate calm, but I can see the tension in her shoulders, the careful way she's avoiding looking in my direction.

"Eliza," I call out, stepping toward her.

She pauses at the door, turning to face me with an expression I've never seen before. Professional. Distant. Like we're strangers who happened to work on a project together.

"Good luck with your new position at Nicholas Industries," she says, her voice perfectly polite and completely empty of warmth. "I'm sure your father knows what's best."

And then she's gone, leaving me standing among my perfect trees, surrounded by my father's business associates discussing market penetration, wondering how everything I worked for just turned into everything I was trying to escape.

11

ELIZA

I WAKE UP ANGRY, WHICH ISN'T UNUSUAL, BUT THIS TIME I can't pinpoint exactly why. Something about last night sits in my stomach like bad cheese, and I keep replaying Reed's presentation while I feed the goats their morning hay.

He was brilliant. Confident, passionate, an extension of the friendly guy who knew half the vendors at the holiday market. Then his father showed up like some smarmy hornet and just... demolished him.

I chuck hay with more force than necessary, making Persephone bleat in protest. "Sorry, girl," I mutter, but I'm not really apologizing to the goat.

I'm pissed that Reed stood there and let his father steamroll him. I'm pissed that he didn't correct the "assistant" thing. But I'm really pissed that I care this much about what some uptight tree scientist does or doesn't say to his daddy.

By 9:00 am, I'm knee-deep in mucking when I hear a truck rumbling up my driveway. I nearly faint with relief at the sight of Martinez, the farrier, showing up for the hoof inspection.

"¡Buenos días, Eliza!" Martinez calls, climbing out of his truck with his usual easy grin. I wonder if he knows he's about to save my ass without compensation. He's wearing those faded jeans that fit him just right and a flannel shirt that brings out his dark eyes.

"About time," I say, but I'm smiling despite my mood. "I was starting to think you'd forgotten about my wee beasties."

"Never," he says, pulling equipment from his truck. "Just been swamped with emergency calls. You know how it is." He doesn't say he's been prioritizing clients who pay, and this classy attitude is another thing I love about him.

Martinez has been our hoof guy since I started, and he's one of the few people who treats my herd like a real business instead of some kind of hobby farm. He's never once made me feel stupid for asking questions, even when I didn't know the difference between hoof rot and laminitis.

I think he's just a few years older than me, and I have no idea what inspires someone to work as an animal foot tender in a major urban area, but he appears to have plenty of work, so who am I to ask questions?

"What's the verdict?" I ask as he approaches the goat pen. "Are my girls going to pass inspection?"

"Let's see." Martinez vaults over the fence with athletic ease, immediately surrounded by curious goats. "Hey there, ladies. Who wants to go first?"

For the next hour, I watch him work his way through my animals with professional efficiency and genuine affection. He checks hooves, files them down, and rubs ointment on some sores. The goats seem to enjoy the attention, which is more than I can say for my own infrequent checkups.

"These animals are in excellent condition," he says, scratching Ursula behind the ears while she tries to eat his stylus. "Whatever you're doing, keep it up."

"Thanks." The relief is immediate and overwhelming. No inspection issues means I can keep the Bramblewood contract, pay Martinez, and maybe even put away a little money for winter. "Nothing terrible about Maleficent's left front hoof?"

"Minor chip, but it's healing well. Nothing to worry about." Martinez moves to the fence, making a final note. "You've got good instincts with these animals, Eliza. A lot of people treat goats like they're lawn mowers with legs, but you understand them."

His hand lands on my shoulder as he says it, warm and friendly, and I realize I'm laughing for the first time since last night's disaster. "Tell that to the city permit office."

"The permit office can kiss my—"

"Eliza?"

We both turn toward the voice. Reed stands at the edge of my driveway, holding a paper bag and wearing an expression I've never seen before. Uncertain. Almost... jealous?

"Reed," I say, suddenly aware that Martinez's hand is on my shoulder. "What are you doing here?"

"I brought something for the goats." He holds up the bag awkwardly. "Organic carrots. As a thank you... for everything."

Martinez glances between us with obvious curiosity. "I'll just finish up my notes," he says diplomatically, moving toward his truck but not quite far enough to be out of earshot.

"You didn't need to do that," I tell Reed, accepting the bag of carrots.

"Yes, I did." Reed's gaze keeps drifting to Martinez, who's pretending to be absorbed in his tablet. "About last night—"

"Don't." I cut him off before he starts apologizing. "Just don't."

"I should have said something. When my father called you my assistant—"

"Reed, stop." I can feel Martinez listening. "It's fine."

It's not fine, but I'm not going to hash this out in front of the farrier.

Reed runs that familiar hand through his hair. "Is that your veterinarian?"

"He's finishing up a hoof inspection." I glance at Martinez, who's definitely eavesdropping. "Martinez, come meet Reed. Reed Saint Nicholas, Alberto Martinez."

"Not my real middle name," Reed insists.

The two men size each other up with the kind of polite wariness men seem to specialize in. Martinez extends a hand first.

"The tree guy," he says with interest. "Eliza mentioned your arrangement. Fascinating."

"Thank you." Reed shakes his hand, but I can see tension in his shoulders. "How long have you been working with Eliza's animals?"

"Years now. Since she first started the business."

Martinez grins. "Watched her build this whole operation from nothing. Pretty impressive woman."

Reed's jaw tightens almost imperceptibly. "Yes, she is."

An awkward silence stretches between them until Martinez clears his throat. "Well, I should check on that donkey before I go." He gestures toward his legs. "I made sure to grab the thick chaps."

I laugh as Reed looks perplexed. "Chiron's protective of me," I tell him as we head toward the donkey's enclosure. "Don't take it personally when he tries to bite you."

Chiron stands in the center of his pen, a furry dictator with ears pinned back and hostile eyes locked on Martinez. When the farrier approaches, Chiron snorts and backs away, shaking his head.

"Easy, big guy," Martinez murmurs, moving slowly. "Nobody's going to hurt you."

Chiron disagrees. Violently.

What follows are ten minutes of the most ridiculous chase scene I've ever witnessed. Martinez tries every trick in the veterinary handbook—treats, gentle coaxing, strategic positioning—while Chiron evades him with the determination of an animal who's offended by the entire concept of medical care.

"Jesus," Martinez pants, leaning against the fence after his latest failed attempt. "That donkey has serious trust issues."

"Tell me about it." Turning to Reed, I add, "He's been like this since I got him. Won't let anyone near him except me, and even then, it's on his terms."

Reed has been watching the whole spectacle with growing interest and moves closer to the fence, studying

Chiron with scientific intensity. "Has he been tested for mineral deficiencies?"

"Uh…" Martinez looks between Reed and me with new respect. "That's a really good question. Eliza?"

"That sounds expensive," I mutter. "He's probably fine."

Martinez shrugs. "You want to hold him for me, so I can at least peek at his feet?"

Martinez and Reed mutter about donkey nutrition as I watch Saint Nicholas transform to the easygoing, quirky guy I hung out with in the greenhouse. Reed knows things about copper and how that affects shiny coats, and Martinez seems impressed. Until Chiron bites him in the thigh, and he leaps out of the pen with a string of Spanish curses.

"Let me try something," Reed says, pulling a carrot from the bag he brought.

"Reed, I really don't think—" I start, but he's already moving toward Chiron.

My demonic donkey, who just spent ten minutes evading a trained animal professional, stands completely still as Reed approaches. No pinned ears. No threatening posture. Just curious attention as Reed extends the carrot through the fence.

Chiron steps forward, sniffs the offering, then gently takes the carrot from Reed's hand.

"Well, I'll be damned," Martinez breathes.

I stare in shock as Chiron allows Reed to scratch his neck, actually leaning into the touch, he's enjoying it with a feline purr. This is the same animal that bit the mailman and refuses to let anyone except me put on his halter.

"Good boy," Reed murmurs, offering another carrot. "You're just misunderstood, aren't you?"

I watch this man I'm supposed to hate sweet-talking my vicious donkey, and there is nothing I can do to stop the flood of heat soaring to my center.

Martinez approaches slowly, and this time Chiron tolerates the examination without protest. Within minutes, Martinez completes his checkup and declared the donkey's feet in perfect health.

Reed steps back from the fence, looking as surprised as the rest of us. After Martinez leaves with reminders about his invoice and the suggestion that we hide vitamins in Chiron's carrots, Reed and I stand by the donkey pen in awkward silence.

"That was..." I search for words. "Chiron doesn't like anyone."

"Maybe he recognizes a fellow outsider," Reed suggests quietly.

Something about the way he says it makes my chest tight. "Reed, about last night—"

"I should have defended you." The words come out rushed, practiced. "When my father called you my assistant, I should have corrected him immediately. You're not my employee, you're..." He trails off, struggling with the words.

"I'm what?"

"You're my friend. You saved my trees, you made the presentation possible, and I let my father dismiss you like you were nobody." Reed's voice gets quieter. "I'm sorry."

The apology hits harder than I expected. "Why didn't you say anything?"

Reed is quiet for a long moment, watching Chiron

munch contentedly on his carrot. "Because when my father talks, I turn into a twelve-year-old kid who just wants his approval. Even when I know he's wrong."

I think about my own mother, the way I avoid her calls and change the subject when my sisters bring her up. The way I've never once told her exactly what I think of her parenting choices, even though I've rehearsed the conversation a thousand times.

"Yeah," I say. "I get that."

My phone buzzes with a text, and I pull it out absent-mindedly.

EDEN

How did the hoof visit go?

I glance at Reed, who's still feeding Chiron carrots like they're old friends.

ME

All good. Animals passed inspection.
Reed showed up and somehow charmed
the devil donkey.

My phone immediately explodes with responses.

EILA

Reed was there??

EVA

Wait, Chiron LIKED him???

ESTHER

That donkey hates everyone except you

EILA

If Chiron approves, that's basically a divine sign

EDEN

Animals can sense people's true nature

EVA

Plus, he gave you a Christmas ornament yesterday and bought you warm nuts??

I stare at the screen, heat creeping up my neck. My sisters have apparently been discussing my love life without me.

It's not like that

EDEN

Sure it's not. Question: is he still coming to the cookie exchange?

I look up at Reed, who's completely absorbed in scratching Chiron's ears. The donkey is practically purring.

"Reed?" I say before I can lose my nerve.

"Mmm?"

"Are you planning to come to my family's cookie exchange?"

He glances up, surprised. "Do you want me to come?"

The honest answer is yes, which terrifies me. "My sisters will never forgive me if I don't bring you."

He smiles, bright and genuine, like I just offered him unlimited candy at the movies. The sight tightens my chest. "Then I'll be there."

As Reed heads to his car, I watch Chiron follow him

to the fence line, clearly hoping for more carrots. My phone buzzes again.

EDEN

Well?

He's coming to cookies

EILA

EXCELLENT

EVA

We're going to love him

ESTHER

If the donkey likes him, we like him

I pocket my phone and look at Chiron, who's staring forlornly after Reed's departing car.

"Yeah," I tell my ridiculous donkey. "I know how you feel."

12

REED

The chocolate chip cookies came out as sad, flat pancakes. I poke one with a fork, and it bounces back.

"How did you manage to make cookies chewy and crunchy at the same time?" Paolo asks, examining the disaster spread across my kitchen counter.

"I followed the recipe exactly," I protest, checking the chocolate chip bag again. "Bake for nine to eleven minutes. I baked for ten."

"Did you measure the flour?" Vick asks, breaking off a piece and immediately spitting it into his napkin.

"Of course I measured. Two and a quarter cups."

Kash holds the measuring cup I used. "Reed, this is in liters. The recipe is in grams."

I stare at the Pyrex cup, then at my friends, then at the cookie graveyard covering every available surface. "There's a difference? I thought there was a 1:1 ratio..."

"Oh, buddy," Paolo says with genuine sympathy. "There's definitely a difference."

Twenty-four cookies that even Eliza's goats would

reject. A cookie exchange where I'm supposed to bring three dozen to share, and I've produced exactly zero edible options.

I text Eliza:

> Can't make it to the exchange. Cookie situation is a disaster.

My phone rings immediately.

"What do you mean you can't make it?" Eliza's voice carries a now-familiar note of irritation.

"I tried to bake cookies. They're inedible. I have nothing to contribute to a cookie exchange."

"So help me bake mine, and I'll share."

I glance around my kitchen, where evidently a flour bomb exploded. "I don't think I'm qualified to help anyone bake anything."

"Reed Saint Nicholas, get your ass over here. I'm making shortbread, and I need someone to knead the dough."

The line goes dead before I can argue—again—that my middle name is not Saint.

Paolo raises his brows as Kash pats me on the back. "This is promising," Kash says. "I think she likes you."

I shake my head, scraping cookie detritus into my trashcan. "Her sisters invited me, and she's beholden."

"Beholden?" Vick arches a dark brow. "She invited you to her house, man."

Paolo holds up a finger. "*Commanded* you to go."

"Best not keep her waiting." Kash shoves me toward the door, and Paolo tosses my car keys. "We'll lock up here."

ELIZA OPENS her door wearing an apron covered in embroidered farm animals. Flour streaks her cheek, and her dark hair is twisted up with a pencil.

"You came," she says, stepping aside to let me in.

"You commanded me to."

"I invited you." She smiles. "Okay, it was a command." Eliza leads me toward the kitchen, which smells of vanilla and butter and everything my kitchen failed to achieve. "Hit me with your best ideas to assembly line this."

Her kitchen is nothing like mine. Mismatched mixing bowls crowd the counter next to containers of ingredients that don't match anything else. A stand mixer that probably dates from the Carter administration whirs in the corner. Mason jars full of flour and sugar sit next to a ceramic cookie jar shaped like a pig.

"This is my grandmother's recipe." She hands me an apron that reads 'Kiss the Cook' in faded letters. "Esther says so, anyway. I don't think any of us met her."

I tie the apron strings, hyperaware of the irony of the message across my chest. "What happened to your grandmother?"

"Mom burned those bridges before I was born." Eliza pulls a chunk of golden dough from her refrigerator. "So we're doing animal shapes, and I think we need twenty-four pointy ears for cats, pink noses for all of them, and I'm not sure how many brown ears for the cows and dogs."

I glance at the few already-shaped cookies lined on parchment paper on the counter. "You made those by hand?" I watch as she transfers the completed cookies to a baking sheet.

"Yeah, and now my fingers are cramped." She hands me a lump of cold dough. "Your job is to work with the orange food coloring and then make me twenty-four tiny triangles. Got it?"

I resist the urge to ask her if they should be isosceles and start poking the dough with my finger. "I can follow directions."

"Good." She grips my bicep and then squeezes it before moving to a bowl of cocoa powder. Heat radiates along my arm where her hand made contact with my sweater.

"Where do you want me?" I ask, then immediately wish I'd phrased that differently.

Eliza's eyes meet mine for a split second before she looks away. "Counter's fine. Just get it nice and even."

For the next hour, we work in a comfortable rhythm as Frank Sinatra croons from an old record player in her living room. I pinch dough into triangles, not caring that my skin dyes orange from the gel.

"These are supposed to be frogs," Eliza says, holding up a lump of green dough she stained with matcha powder.

"They look like Christmas trees to me."

"Reed, they have four legs."

"Pine trees. Definitely pine trees." I position the shape at an angle. "See? Perfect evergreen silhouette."

"You're impossible." But she's smiling as she says it, and when our hips bump as we work around each other, neither of us moves away.

"This is nice," I say, surprising myself.

"What is?"

"This. Your house. It feels…" I search for the right word. "Lived in."

Eliza glances around her kitchen, taking in mismatched everything and flour handprints on cabinet doors. "It's kind of a mess."

"It's perfect." Everything in my apartment matches and looks like it came from a catalog. This kitchen looks like people cook here, live here. "My place feels like a hotel room."

"Probably a really nice hotel room."

"Probably. But this feels like a home."

Something shifts in her expression, softer than I've seen before. "Help me clean up?"

I nod and walk to the sink as Eliza slides pans of cookies into her massive oven to bake. I'm elbow-deep in soapy water when she turns to dust off her hands, staring.

"What?" I ask.

"You're washing dishes."

"Did you expect me to leave them for you?"

"Honestly? Yeah." She leans against the counter. "Most guys I know think kitchen cleanup happens by magic."

"My parents have household staff," I admit, scrubbing a mixing bowl. "But I also told you I can follow instructions."

"I guess you meant that."

I rinse a bowl and hand it to her. "I definitely did."

Eliza's quiet for a moment, methodically drying the bowl. "What made you start a wonky tree business? Since you're such a rule follower…"

I drain the sink and turn to face her. "I don't know," I

admit. "I finished my master's program and didn't like most of the options I saw in bioengineering." I shrug. "It just sort of happened."

Eliza's face brightens as she snaps a lid onto a metal tin full of amazing cookies. "That's how I got into urban goat work." She laughs. "Definitely not something I wrote as a life goal in elementary school."

I lean to glance at the other pans of perfect cookies. "Turned out okay, though. Right?"

She nods, and we're both quiet as the Sinatra record finishes. I've lost track of how many times we listened through. The air is warm and thick with the scent of butter and vanilla. Eliza's kitchen is a safe little incubator.

For some reason, amidst the cozy comfort, I blurt, "My father threatened to make sure no serious investor in Pittsburgh will touch my business if I don't join Nicholas Industries."

Her eyes flash with anger. "He can do that?"

"He thinks he can. Charles Nicholas has a long memory and an extensive network." The words taste bitter. "He's probably right."

"That's horseshit." Eliza tosses a dishtowel onto the counter with more force than necessary. "Your trees are brilliant. Anyone with half a brain can see the potential."

"Not brilliant enough for anyone to risk losing a contract with Nicholas Industries."

"What about investors outside of Pittsburgh? Or finding people who don't give a damn what your father thinks? My sisters know people." She steps close enough that I can see gold flecks in her brown eyes. "You can't let him win."

The conviction in her voice does something to my

chest, makes it tight and warm simultaneously. "You really believe that?"

"I believe in you."

The words hang between us, simple and devastating. I step closer, drawn by her fierce loyalty and the way she's looking at me like I'm worth fighting for.

"Eliza..." I reach up to brush flour from her cheek.

A tremendous bray erupts from outside, followed by the unmistakable thump of Chiron attacking the side of the house. We spring apart, both of us laughing despite the interrupted moment.

"That ass has terrible timing," Eliza mutters, but she won't quite meet my eyes.

"Or perfect timing," I mumble.

Because if that donkey hadn't interrupted us, I would have kissed her. And once I started, I'm not sure I would have been able to stop.

13

ELIZA

I STARE AT THE DOOR REED DISAPPEARED THROUGH WHEN headlights sweep across my kitchen window. I hear laughter and van doors closing, which means trouble in the form of my meddling sisters.

Eden and Eila tumble through my front door without knocking, Eden carrying a six-pack of glass bottles and Eila oozing a drunken aura.

"We brought the prototype," Eila announces as Eden sets the bottles on my counter with ceremony. "Honey hop beer. Eden's wildflower honey with my cascade hops."

"It's nine o'clock," I point out.

"Perfect time for alcohol," Eden says, then stops mid-step. "Holy shit, Liza. You decorated."

I follow her gaze around my living room, seeing it through her eyes. The scattered evergreen boughs rest on the mantle. String lights wind around the window frames. The wooden goat ornament Reed gave me sits prominently on the coffee table next to the containers of animal cookies.

"It's nothing," I mutter.

"It's definitely something." Eila pokes at the record player, which is still spinning Frank Sinatra. "Since when do you listen to crooner music?"

"Since I felt like it."

Eden opens one of the bottles, using her silver bangle to pop the cap and pours three small glasses of amber liquid. "This smells incredible." She glances toward my kitchen window where I've set up a small hydroponic herb garden. "When did you start growing basil indoors?"

"Reed mentioned the setup was simple for herbs." The words slip out before I can stop them. "Someone was giving away the countertop thing on Buy Nothing."

My sisters exchange a look loaded with enough meaning to power the city grid.

"*Reed* mentioned..." Eila repeats slowly.

"It was just a suggestion."

"Uh-huh." Eden hands me a glass. "How is Tree Boy?"

"Fine." I take a sip of the beer, which is amazing—the honey rounds out the hoppy bite perfectly. "This is good."

"Don't change the subject," Eila says, settling onto my couch with obvious plans to stay awhile. "Spill."

"There's nothing to spill. We made cookies for tomorrow's exchange. He helped with the dishes. End of story."

"Really?" Eden perches on the arm of my ancient recliner. "Because you've got flour in your hair and you're glowing. I'm thinking you just got properly kissed."

Heat creeps up my neck. "I am not glowing."

"You are definitely glowing," Eila confirms. "Also, you never put up decorations. Ever. Remember last year when Eva begged you to hang a spiderweb for

Halloween, and you told her holidays are a capitalist conspiracy?"

"Maybe I changed my mind."

"Maybe Saint Nicholas changed your mind." Eden grins.

I take another sip of beer, buying time. "It's not like that."

"What's it like?" Eila asks.

I stare into my glass, trying to find words for something I don't understand myself. "It's complicated."

"Most good things are," Eden says.

"He's not like I thought."

"How so?"

"He listens when I talk about my work. He doesn't act like what I do is cute or quaint." I set my glass down harder than necessary. "He washed dishes without being asked."

"The bar is so low for men," Eila mutters.

"But he cleared it," Eden adds. "That's something."

I want to tell them about the way he looked at my kitchen in awe, about his vulnerability when he talked about his father, about the moment before Chiron interrupted when I thought he might kiss me. Instead, I say, "He's Reed Saint Nicholas."

"Meaning what?" Eila asks.

"Meaning he's rich. Dynasty rich. His family owns half of the development projects in the county, and he thinks he's some sort of do-gooder saint, bringing the gift of trees to bougie people in condos." I stand, suddenly restless. "What am I supposed to do with that?"

"Enjoy it?" Eden suggests. "I sell a lot of my honey

and beeswax products to those condo dwellers." My sister shrugs.

"It's not that simple." I pace toward the window, looking at the goat pen where Chiron stands sentinel in the darkness. "He holds all the power here."

"What do you mean?" Eila asks.

"He's the one who decides whether I'm free and clear of the fifteen thousand dollars in damages." The words taste bitter. "Technically, he could still sue me if he wanted to."

My sisters go quiet, and I can practically hear them processing this information.

"But he wouldn't," Eden says. "I mean, you've been helping him, he obviously likes you—"

"Obviously?" I laugh, but there's no humor in it. "What's obvious is I destroyed his work, and I'm in his debt. Who even knows if he's been telling the truth about his shitty parents. Could be feeding me a line because he saw my soft spots."

"Eliza, that's not—" Eila starts.

"Isn't it?" I turn to face them. "Think about it. I help him fix his trees, I help him make cookies for my family's party, I make him look good in front of people he wants to impress. And in return, he doesn't destroy my credit and my business."

"You're being paranoid," Eden says firmly.

"Am I? What do we know about him except that he comes from money? We have a lot of experience with how rich people treat people like us." I take a gulp of beer, feeling the impact of the strong ale.

Eila shifts. "Ben happened to notice some amendments to Reed's business filings this week. He was curious about what they might be about."

My stomach drops. "What kind of amendments?"

"He didn't know. Just that something had been updated with the city. You know how Ben is about paperwork."

"See?" I gesture broadly. "Reed's changing things. Probably covering his ass before he cuts me loose and sicks his lawyer on me."

"Or maybe he finally figured out the paperwork forms you said he was struggling with," Eden suggests.

I snort. "Yeah right."

Eila counters, "What's that they say about the simplest answer making the most sense?"

I down the rest of my beer in one gulp. The honey and hops do nothing to settle my churning thoughts. "I should have known better than to trust someone like him."

"Someone like him?" Eden's voice sharpens. "Someone who brought carrots for your goats and charmed your psychotic donkey?"

"Someone who has the power to ruin me."

"Jesus, Liza," Eila says. "What did Mom do to you?"

The question hits like a slap. "This isn't about Mom."

"Isn't it? You're so terrified of being hurt that you're sabotaging something good before it even starts."

"I'm being realistic. Just because you two found perfect men doesn't mean the rest of them aren't shitty monsters."

"You're scared," Eden says. "And I get it. But Reed isn't Mom. Why not give him a chance?"

I collect their glasses, needing something to do with

my hands. "A chance to wreck my credit and crush my business? No thanks. I need to rein it in and sever ties."

"The cookie exchange is tomorrow," Eden says. "He's coming, right?"

"I don't know. Maybe I should tell him not to."

"Maybe you should give him a chance," Eila suggests.

AFTER THEY LEAVE, I sit in my decorated living room, listening to the record player skip on the last song. The wooden goat Reed gave me stares at me from the coffee table, and I can't decide if it represents something beginning or something I'm about to ruin.

The truth is, I've been waiting for the other shoe to drop since the moment I realized I cared about him. Rich guys don't end up with women like me—women who have trust issues and get along better with goats than dinner companions.

But what if I'm wrong? I think about how he acted at the market, the way his friends tease him about being uptight. It reminded me of how my sisters and I act when we're together. Someone with a tight network can't be a slimy creep, right?

The question that really terrifies me: am I brave enough to find out?

REED

"I THINK I'M FALLING FOR HER," I ADMIT, STARING INTO MY pint of Perfect Storm IPA in search of answers.

Paolo nearly chokes on his beer. "The goat lady?"

"Her name is Eliza," I say firmly. "And yes."

Kash raises his glass. "About time you admitted it. You've been mooning over her."

I scoff. "Who even says mooning?"

"You absolutely have been pining," Vick adds. "You asked me five separate times if I thought she liked the ornament you bought her."

The three of them exchange knowing looks across our usual table at Three Rivers Brewing. "So, what's the problem?" Paolo asks. "She obviously likes you, too. Chiron the demon donkey approves." He takes a swig of beer. "And she's hot, right? Seems like a win all around."

I know my friend is just making observations, but I realize I don't like thinking he's been looking at Eliza. Which is dumb macho thinking. But there my brain goes, and suddenly I'm thinking about the glimpse I caught of her bra when she was rigging up lights in the greenhouse. Not to mention the pinch of jealousy I felt flood my central nervous system when I saw her with the hoof guy. I tap my fingers on the table. "The problem is, I'm terrified I'm going to screw it up."

I take a long sip of my drink, appreciating the storm-themed flavor names as I sit and ponder my own storm of a problem. "Tomorrow I'm meeting her entire family, and I have no idea how to act around normal people."

"What do you mean, normal people?" Kash asks.

"People who like each other? People who say what they mean? I don't know... people who don't analyze every conversation for hidden meanings and power dynamics."

Vick laughs. "Reed, you are literally sitting at a table surrounded by friends."

"That's different."

"How?"

I struggle to find words for the distinction that feels so obvious to me. "You basically have to be nice to me."

Kash snorts. "I definitely do not."

Vick punches him in the arm, and Paolo gestures for me to continue. I scratch my head. "Eliza is... genuine. Real. When she talks about her goats, she lights up with joy. When she problem-solves, she just does it. No committees or feasibility studies or risk assessments. But she's aggressively confident about all of it."

"So basically, you're attracted to someone who's nothing like your parents," Paolo observes.

The accuracy of that statement hits harder than I expected. "When you put it like that..."

"It's not a bad thing," Kash says. "Your parents are

corporate sharks who think empathy is a weakness. Finding someone who's the opposite makes sense."

"What if I'm just rebelling? What if this is some psychological reaction to my upbringing?"

"Or..." Vick suggests, "what if you're just a person who knows what makes you happy, and you're finally brave enough to pursue it?"

I consider this, watching condensation drip down my glass. "I'm not brave. If I were brave, I would have told my father to shove his job offer instead of standing there like a statue while he humiliated me."

My friends are quiet enough for me to hear the holiday music piping through the bar. Our server, dressed in an elf costume, comes to clear our empty glasses, and I realize we've been here a long time. This place feels like home in a way my apartment never has, probably because it's full of people who choose to be here rather than people obligated by blood or business connections.

"So, what's your plan for tomorrow?" Vick asks.

"Survive," I say. "Try not to say anything that reveals how privileged and out of touch I am. Hope her family doesn't decide I'm too much of a risk."

"Risk?" Paolo's eyebrows go up.

"Risk to Eliza. Risk of hurting her." I finish my beer and signal the server for another round. "Her sisters are protective. If they think I'm manipulating them..."

"Are you manipulating them?" Kash asks.

The question stops me cold. "Of course not." I stare at my friends. "But I don't know how to do this. I always mess things up with women."

"Worrying about how she feels is probably a good sign," Vick observes. "Means it matters."

The elf announces last call, so we order a round of Thunder Struck and move to discuss everything except my love life—Paolo's trip to Colombia for Christmas, Vick's mother yearning for grandchildren, Kash explaining to his parents yet again that Solstice is different from the Lunar New Year.

My thoughts keep drifting to Eliza. The way she laughs, how it sounds a little like a donkey... The fierce concentration on her face when she's working. The softness in her voice when she talked me through cat cookie assembly.

By the time the guys drop me at home, I'm slightly buzzed and completely overthinking tomorrow.

What does one wear to a family cookie exchange? My usual button-down and khakis feel too formal, but jeans might be too casual. Do I bring something to go with the cookies? Should I offer to help with cleanup? What if they ask about my family? What if they already know about my father's public humiliation of me?

I SLEEP FITFULLY AND, in the morning, I pull half my wardrobe out of the closet, trying to find something that says "responsible adult who cares about your sister" without screaming "trust fund baby who's never done a real day's work."

A simple sweater, maybe? The navy one that Paolo says brings out my eyes? Or is that trying too hard?

By the time I decide on dark jeans and a forest green

Henley—casual but not sloppy, approachable but not desperate—it's past ten, and I should have been at Esther's house twenty minutes ago.

I grab a carton of nonalcoholic eggnog since I didn't have time to age the good kind, check my reflection one more time, and drive across town with my stomach in knots.

Esther Storm's house glows with warm light, and I can hear laughter and conversation through the windows. Multiple cars line the street of colorful homes, and there's a hand-painted sign out front that says STORM CHALET. It strikes me—it's a really big deal to be invited here.

I park at the end of the block and walk back, rehearsing casual greetings in my head. The December air is crisp and clear, and the yards on this block have inflatable decorations with kitschy homemade paper snowflakes in the windows. This was set up by the actual people who live here, not hired professional decorators aiming for classy one-upmanship.

It looks like a Christmas card, the kind of family gathering I've seen in movies but never experienced.

I'm halfway up the front walk when Eliza's voice carries through the storm door.

"I think it's a mistake," she's saying, her tone sharp with frustration. "Getting involved with someone like him. Someone who holds that much power over my life."

My hand freezes inches from the doorbell.

"Someone like him always gets what they want," she continues. "And when they're done, people like us get left with the wreckage."

The eggnog suddenly feels impossibly heavy in my hands.

15

———

ELIZA

THE STORM CHALET IS IN FULL CHAOS WHEN I HEAR THE doorbell, which means Reed is twenty minutes late. I'm balancing three different conversations—Eva asking about goat cheese photos, Ben explaining municipal composting regulations to anyone who'll listen, and Koa trying to convince Esther that her gingerbread recipe needs rum—when Esther opens the front door.

"You must be Reed," she says warmly. "Come in, come in. We're just getting started."

I turn from where I'm arranging cookies on platters to find Reed looking like someone just told him his hydroponic system caught fire. Of course, he probably heard me talking about him before he walked in. Now I feel like shit and stole the sparkle in his smile.

"Sorry I'm late," he says, offering Esther a carton of eggnog. His voice has that careful, polite tone people use when they're trying very hard not to show they're upset.

"No worries at all," Esther says, but I catch her

glancing at me with raised eyebrows. "Let me introduce you to everyone."

Reed nods and follows her into the living room, but something's wrong. His shoulders are tense, his smile looks painted, and when Eva bounces over to hug him—because Eva hugs everyone—he accepts it like he's bracing for impact.

"Reed!" Eden beams. "Perfect timing. We're about to start the gingerbread house competition."

"Great," Reed says, and it's the least enthusiastic 'great' I've ever heard.

I abandon my cookie arranging and approach him, studying his face. I should apologize. I should pull him aside to talk. What comes out of my mouth is, "Hey, you okay?"

His gaze meets mine for just a second before sliding away. "Fine. Just tired."

He's lying. Reed's a terrible liar—his jaw does this twitching thing when he's not telling the truth, and it's twitching now like Morse code. He's acting like he did when his father was ruining his investor pitch.

"Are you sure? You seem—"

"I'm fine, Eliza." The words come out sharp, and now everyone in the room is looking at us.

Ben, bless his awkward heart, chooses this moment to launch into an explanation of sustainable packaging, giving me cover to pull Reed aside.

"I need to talk to you," I whisper.

"Everything's fine." Reed straightens his shoulders, transforming into the polite, controlled person I met at the permit office. "Are we doing the contest?"

Before I can press him further, Eva appears with a

toolkit of decorating supplies and an expression of pure competitive joy.

"Reed, you're on my team," she announces. "We're going to destroy Eliza and Koa."

"Teams are already decided?" Reed asks, and I swear there's relief in his voice at the distraction.

"Eva's been planning your strategy for an hour," Koa says with a grin. "She's taking this very seriously."

"Good," Reed says, and this time his smile looks almost genuine. "I like winning."

THE NEXT HOUR passes in a blur of frosting, candy, and increasingly ridiculous architecture. Eva and Reed work with scientific precision, measuring angles and testing structural integrity before placing each gingerbread shingle. From what I can see, Eva is mostly taking photos for her online accounts while Reed acts like he's in his hydroponic lab. Koa and I go for artistic flair over engineering, which means our house looks charming but leans at an alarming angle.

"Your roof is going to collapse," Eva observes, carefully piping icing along the perfectly straight roofline Reed constructed.

"Your house has no personality," I counter, adding another gumball to our whimsical chimney.

Reed, I notice, seems to relax as he absorbs in the competition. He and Eva develop an easy rapport, with him calculating load-bearing walls while she provides color commentary that has everyone laughing.

"Reed, you're like a gingerbread engineer," Eden says,

watching him reinforce a corner with mathematical precision. She and Nate made a gingerbread beehive, predictable and boring, and are now mostly eating and heckling.

"I prefer 'confectionery architect,'" he says solemnly, which gets a genuine laugh from the room.

This is the Reed I've gotten to know—funny, smart, a little obsessive about details but in an endearing way. So why did he arrive looking like someone had kicked his dog? I realize he could have heard me bitching about his family right before his arrival, and a mess of emotion knots in my stomach. I didn't say anything I wasn't thinking, but I also would probably offer Reed more context if he and I were sparring over hydroponic fluid.

"Time!" Esther calls, and we all step back to admire our creations.

Eva and Reed's house looks magazine-ready—perfect proportions, elegant decoration, structurally sound. It's the sort of place I imagine Reed grew up in. Koa's and my house looks like a cottage designed by someone on hallucinogens, but it has character. Eden's beehive is boring as hell, and Esther makes sure to point that out as she and Ben feed their collapsed structure to his dog, Maurice.

"We win on technical merit," Eva says smugly.

"We win on artistic vision," I counter.

"You win on most likely to be condemned by the building inspector," Ben adds helpfully.

As everyone argues about judging criteria, I catch Reed watching me with an expression I can't quite read. There's something sad about it, like he's memorizing this moment for later.

"What?" I whisper.

"Nothing," he says, but his smile doesn't reach his eyes. "Just enjoying the chaos." He munches a cookie. "I never asked what the winner gets. Is there a prize?"

I arch a brow. "Prize?"

He recoils a bit, like he's said something dumb. "Don't contests usually have prizes?" He looks around for validation, but everyone is busy squabbling.

"Reed." I sigh and pat his arm. "The prize is the gloating. Knowing you've dominated. Queen of the Storms."

My sisters and their significant others come to a surly agreement, and Esther bangs a spoon on her glass of nog. "All right, everyone. We have chosen a winner."

Eden smiles. "I hope nobody acts mean this year. We all made really nice structures." She pats her hive lovingly, and I squint, noticing it doesn't budge under her touch. Did she cheat and use real glue?

Koa points a thick finger in Reed's direction and raises a glass in his direction. "Eva and our new contender are the winners." The room echoes with a collective gasp. "Cheers, mate." Koa claps Reed on the back as he visibly works to hold in a gloating celebration. Eva does nothing to contain herself, whooping and hip-checking Reed until he howls and bumps into the table, toppling their so-called winning construction as everyone devolves into laughter.

The party winds down gradually, with everyone taking cardboard boxes full of cookies. There's a moment of exasperated hooting when Reed realizes Eila is the brewer behind his favorite new IPA.

Reed smacks himself on the forehead. "Eye of the Storm. Perfect Storm. I should have guessed once I met Eliza."

Eila beams. "You're a beer guy, eh? Eliza made it sound like you only drink iced Chilean chardonnay."

Reed's smile fades, and Eila winces, tugging Ben out the door with promises to bring Reed a sample of the honey ale.

Eva loads the dishwasher while Esther wraps leftovers, leaving Reed and me to tackle the gingerbread debris covering her dining room table.

"Your family is awesome," Reed says, carefully scraping hardened frosting off the tablecloth.

"They're loud," I say.

"They care about each other. It shows." He's quiet for a moment.

"Reed..." I start, but Esther appears with a garbage bag.

"You two are saints for cleaning up," she says. "Eliza, walk Reed to his car. I'll finish this."

I want to argue, but Esther has a tone that means the discussion is over. So, I grab my jacket and follow Reed outside into the cold December air.

"Thank you," he says when we reach his car. "For including me today. Your family is... They're really special."

"They like you," I say, which is true. Eva spent ten minutes explaining her online presence to him, and even Koa—who's protective of all of us—seemed charmed by Reed's earnest questions about plant life in New Zealand.

"Did they?" Reed asks, and something in his voice makes my chest tight.

"Of course they did. Why wouldn't they?"

He doesn't answer, just unlocks his car and turns to face me. In the porch light, his eyes look impossibly sad.

"Reed, what's—"

Before I can finish the question, something compels me to step closer and press my lips to his cheek. It's meant to be a friendly gesture, a thank-you for being so good with my family despite whatever's bothering him.

But when my lips touch his skin, everything changes. His breath catches, his hand comes up to rest lightly on my waist, and suddenly we're standing much too close in the winter air.

I pull back, flustered, and Reed's looking at me with an expression of such hope and confusion that it makes my heart race.

"Goodnight," I say quickly, backing toward the house.

"Eliza, wait—"

But I'm already at the front door, fumbling with the handle and definitely not looking back at his car as he drives away.

Inside, Esther's waiting with two cups of tea and a knowing expression.

"So," she says, settling onto the couch. "Want to tell me why that boy looked like someone stole his lunch money?"

I sink into the chair across from her, touching my lips where I can still feel the warmth of his cheek. "I have no idea."

The lie tastes bitter, because I have a terrible feeling I do know. And if I'm right, I've just made everything infinitely more complicated.

16

ELIZA

I spend Sunday night and Monday morning replaying Reed's face when he left Esther's house. That expression of hope and confusion, like he wanted to believe something good might happen but couldn't quite trust it.

I know that feeling.

By midmorning, I've fed the goats, mucked stalls, and run out of excuses to avoid what I need to do. Reed looked destroyed at the cookie exchange, and I'm pretty sure I know why. The timing of his mood shift, the way he went all polite and distant—he heard me talking about "someone like him" before he knocked.

Which means I hurt him, and despite all my fears about rich boys and power dynamics, the thought of Reed thinking I see him as some entitled asshole makes my stomach twist. Even more after the way he acted with my family. He folded right into our tornado.

I load Chiron and the girls into the trailer and head to the ivy-covered warehouse Reed hooked me up with, telling myself I'm just doing my job. I am unable to let go of my guilt, but when I get the goats situated to finish their work —with a duly reinforced fence—instead of heading home, I drive north to the Sustainable Innovation Incubator.

Reed's car sits in the parking lot, so I know he's here. I sit in my truck for five minutes, trying to figure out what I'm going to say.

> Hey, sorry you overheard me having a breakdown about my trust issues?

Delete.

> Want to discuss how my abandonment issues make me sabotage good things?

Delete.

> Sorry I'm a mess who can't tell the difference between genuine connection and potential exploitation?

No fucking way.

Finally, I get out and walk to his greenhouse.

Reed's hunched over a tray of seedlings, wearing a forest green Henley that really works for him. His hair looks adorably disheveled, and there are coffee rings on his worktable suggesting he's been here a while.

"Reed," I say, knocking on the doorframe.

He looks up, and his expression goes carefully neutral. "Eliza. Is everything okay?"

"Yeah." I step inside, closing the door behind me. "I wanted to talk to you."

"About what?" His tone is polite, professional, distant... everything I was afraid of.

"About yesterday. About how you seemed upset." I take a breath. "About what you must have heard before you knocked on Esther's door."

Reed goes stills. "I don't know what you mean."

"Yes, you do." I move closer, noting how he doesn't quite meet my eyes. "You heard me talking to my sisters. About getting involved with *someone like you*."

He sets down his tablet. "I heard enough."

"Reed—"

"It's fine, Eliza." His voice is steady, controlled. "You were being realistic. I appreciate honesty."

"No, you don't understand. I wasn't—" I struggle for words. "That wasn't about you specifically. That was about me being terrified."

"Of me."

"Of caring about you." The words come out in a rush. "Of letting myself trust someone who could destroy my life if they wanted to."

Reed finally looks at me directly. "I would never—"

"I know that. Logically, I know that." I pace the rows of trees, needing to move. "But my mother spent my entire childhood making me promises she had no intention of keeping. She'd show up with grand plans and stories about how things were going to be different, and I believed her every single time. Until the next time she inevitably disappeared."

"Eliza…"

"So, when I started caring about you—really caring— my brain went into full panic mode." I turn to face him. "Because if you decided I wasn't worth the trouble, if you got bored or found someone more suitable or just remembered you're Reed Nicholas and I'm the goat lady who destroyed your trees—"

"Stop." Reed steps closer, his jaw tight. "Just stop."

"I don't think you're a bad person. I'm damaged goods who doesn't know how to trust without waiting for the other shoe to drop."

"You're not damaged." His voice is fierce, certain.

The conviction in his words nearly undoes me. "Reed, I'm sorry. For what you heard, for how I made you feel..."

"You were protecting yourself." He runs a hand through his hair. "I get it. I do. But hearing you talk about me like I'm some kind of threat—"

"You're not a threat. You're the opposite of a threat." I step closer, close enough to see the gold flecks in his eyes. "You're kind and genuine, and you make me want to be braver than I am."

"Just so you know, you aren't the only emotionally stunted tree in this forest." He shakes his head. "My parents did a number on me, too. And..." He blows out a breath. "It stung hearing you talk about me as if I'm like them."

I smile. "I guess we're a fucked-up pair."

He purses his lips. "Yeah." He meets my eye over the top of his glasses, and the sight sends tingles to my lower abdomen. "And I like you, anyway."

I can feel him waiting for me to respond, to tell him I like him, too, to hold his hand and pick up where we left off in my kitchen.

I wince. "I just can't get past the fact that I'm indebted to you, Reed. The liability thing. The thousands of dollars—"

"Oh, that?" His face brightens, and Reed strides to his desk, pulling out a manila folder. "Here."

He hands me a sheet of paper with an official-looking letterhead. I scan the typed paragraph with bolded phrases: **Reed Nicholas** of **Urban Forest Solutions** hereby releases **Eliza Storm** of **Mobile Urban Natural Clearing Herd** from all liability related to the incident of November 15th...

"You're releasing me from the debt," I say, staring at the paper.

He watches my face. "The damage was an accident. You've more than made up for it by helping me recover in time for the pitch. I never, ever want you to feel you owe me anything."

"Reed..." I look up at him, this man who's been quietly protecting me while I've been spinning paranoid fantasies about his motives.

"Sign it," he says. "Then we're equals. No power imbalance, no debt, no obligation. Just two people deciding if they want to... go to a fancy party together."

I sign my name with a shaky hand, and when I look up, Reed is watching me with an expression so hopeful it makes my chest tight.

"Now what?" I ask.

"Now I acknowledge I have never done a prom-posal, and I ask you if you'll be my date for the Yule Gala. If you think Mandy Warnick will let us back on the premises."

I'm about to laugh and tell him yes when the greenhouse's automatic sprinkler system activates with a mechanical whir. Water rains down on us from multiple directions, soaking through my jacket in seconds.

"Shit!" Reed lunges for the control panel. "The timer must be malfunctioning—"

But I'm laughing, because of course this would happen. Of course, the universe would choose this moment to drench us both. Reed's Henley clings to his chest, water dripping from his hair, and when he turns to me, his eyes drop to where my wet t-shirt has become essentially transparent.

His gaze lingers on my chest for just a moment—not long enough to be inappropriate, but long enough for me to see exactly what he's thinking. When his eyes meet mine again, there's heat there that has nothing to do with embarrassment.

"Eliza," he says, his voice rough.

The way he's looking at me—like he wants to touch me, taste me, take me apart and put me back together—sends panic shooting through my system. This is real. This attraction, this connection, this thing between us that's been building for weeks.

I'm terrified of how much I want it.

"I have to go," I say quickly, backing toward the door.

"Wait—"

But I'm already fleeing again, leaving Reed standing in his flooded greenhouse with water dripping from his hair and that same expression of hope and confusion I've seen too many times.

I make it to my truck before I allow myself to look back. Through the greenhouse windows, I can see Reed standing exactly where I left him, watching me drive away. I guess this has nothing to do with me owing him money and everything to do with what I thought earlier: my mother has fucked me up beyond repair. I can't be anyone's sweetheart. I'm not Yule Gala material because I have nothing emotional to offer. And Reed Nicholas deserves the kind of girl who can bang him against one of his tree trunks *and* support him with all the other stuff in a relationship.

It's better that the universe threw cold water on this before we caught fire.

17

REED

THE WEATHER APP ON MY PHONE SHOWS AN ANGRY RED blob moving toward Pittsburgh, complete with warnings about ice accumulation and power outages. I tell myself I'm checking road conditions because I need to get home safely before the storm hits.

I'm definitely not thinking about Eliza.

Except I am. I've been thinking about her for the past six hours, replaying the moment she signed that liability release and the way her face lit up when I asked her to the Yule Gala. Then the sprinklers went off, and she looked at me like I was something dangerous and bolted.

Again.

The rational part of my brain knows she's dealing with abandonment issues. The irrational part wonders if I can somehow plead my case that we can try to be together. God, even thinking it sounds pathetic.

My phone buzzes with a severe weather alert just as Paolo texts the group chat:

Roads are getting bad. Everyone go buy bread and toilet paper, STAT.

I laugh, knowing I should go to my apartment, defrost something, and wait out the storm like a sensible person. Instead, I drive toward Eliza's neighborhood, telling myself I'm just concerned about her animals in this weather.

Which is partly true, but mostly, I'm worried about her.

The roads get progressively worse as I head uphill to her neighborhood, snow beginning to mix with sleet, tinkling as it all hits my windshield. This is Pittsburgh, so of course the roads haven't been pre-treated. By the time I reach Eliza's driveway, my car is sliding more than driving.

I park behind her truck and see her wrestling with the trailer gate, trying to coax Chiron down the ramp while snow swirls around them. The donkey plants his feet and refuses to budge, ears pinned against the wind.

"Come on, you stubborn ass," Eliza yells over the weather. "It's warm inside!"

I approach carefully, not wanting to spook either of them. "Need help?"

Eliza whips around, her face a mix of surprise and possibly relief. "What are you doing here?"

"Thought you might need extra hands getting everyone secure."

She eyes me suspiciously, snow collecting on her knit hat. "You drove out here in this weather to help with goats?"

"I really love ruminants," I say, which makes her snort.

"Chiron's not technically a ruminant."

"I love equids, too."

That gets me an almost-smile before she turns to the donkey. "He's being dramatic about the ice. Thinks he's going to slip."

I study the situation—Chiron's wide stance, the way he's eyeing the ramp, the patches of ice forming on the trailer floor. "He's not wrong. That ramp is getting slick."

"What do you suggest, Dr. Dolittle?"

I grab the bag of goat manure I've had in my trunk for the past two weeks since she and I argued about it. I scatter it on the truck bed and ramp, creating, if not traction exactly, a familiar-smelling surface I hope Chiron will trust.

He sniffs the poop, takes a tentative step, then walks down like it was his idea all along.

"Oh yeah." I pump my fist and shoot finger guns at the donkey, like he and I won some sort of contest.

"Show off," Eliza mutters, but she's smiling.

For the next hour, Eliza lets me help her. She directs while I follow orders, which is pretty hot. We check on the animals' bedding, fill their water troughs, and make sure they have enough hay.

We move around each other carefully, both hyper-aware of the other's presence.

The physical work feels good, purposeful. This is what a partnership should look like, I think. Two people working toward the same goal, complementing each other's strengths. I feel useful here in her space, like she was in mine.

"Last load," Eliza calls, gesturing toward a stack of hay bales around the back of the barn.

I grab two bales, muscles straining against the weight. The snow is coming down harder now, and ice has formed a treacherous layer over everything. I'm three steps from the door when my foot hits a slick patch.

Physics takes over. Again.

The hay bales go flying as I crash hard, my right ankle twisting beneath me at an angle that definitely isn't natural. Pain shoots up my leg, sharp and immediate.

"Reed!" Eliza drops her own bale and rushes over. "Are you okay?"

"Fine," I grit out, trying to stand. The ankle immediately buckles, sending another wave of pain through my system. "Shit."

"Don't move." Eliza kneels beside me in the snow, her hands gentle as she examines my ankle. "Can you wiggle your toes?"

I try, wincing. "Yeah."

"Good. Probably not broken." Her face creases with concern. "Can you put any weight on it?"

I try again, managing to stand with most of my weight on my left foot. "Not really." Walking is going to be interesting.

"Come on," Eliza says, sliding under my arm to support me. "Let's get you inside."

"I should go home—"

"Reed, look around." She gestures at the weather, which has turned into a proper storm... and not the sexy woman variety. "Nobody's driving anywhere tonight."

She's right. Visibility is maybe ten feet, and the roads will be impassable by now. Our phones both start beeping with an emergency weather alert, like a punctuation mark on this disaster of a day.

"You can take over my couch," Eliza says as we make our slow progress toward the house. "It's not much, but it's warm and dry."

"I don't want to impose—"

"Reed, you literally just hurt yourself helping me take care of my animals. The least I can do is give you somewhere to wait out the blizzard."

As always, her house feels like a refuge from the chaos outside. Eliza settles me on the couch with ice wrapped in a dish towel for my ankle, then disappears into the kitchen. I hear her moving around—opening cabinets, running water, and the gentle clink of dishes.

"Cocoa?" she calls.

"Please."

She returns with two steaming mugs and settles into the chair across from me. "I wish I had warm nuts." She shrugs. I fight the urge to make a joke. The silence stretches, filled with the sounds of wind howling outside and tree branches scraping the roof.

"Thank you," I say. "For letting me stay."

"Thank you for helping with the girls." Eliza wraps her hands around her mug. "You didn't have to do that."

"I wanted to help."

"Why?"

The question catches me off guard. "Because I care about you and your ridiculous villains."

She studies my face as if she's trying to solve a puzzle. "Reed, about earlier, at the greenhouse—"

The lights flicker once. Twice.

Then everything goes dark.

"Well," Eliza's voice comes through the darkness, dry and amused. "This should be interesting."

In the sudden silence, with the familiar hum of electricity gone, I can hear my own heartbeat. And somewhere in the darkness, Eliza's breathing.

18

REED

"Stay put," Eliza's voice cuts through the blackout. "I'm getting a candle."

I hear her moving around, muttering, and then a match strikes. The room fills with warm light as she places a candle on the table, then another, and then a small altar's worth of votives.

"Very romantic," I say, then immediately wish I hadn't.

"Very practical," she corrects, but I catch the hint of a smile in her voice. "I steal leftovers from Eden. They're beeswax."

I watch her shuffle to a squat woodstove in the corner, open the door, and work on lighting it. Within minutes, she's got a fire crackling, and I immediately feel the warmth.

"Better?" she asks.

"Much." I watch her move around her house, closing curtains against the storm, adjusting candles. "You're good at this."

"Practice." She settles into her chair, but there's tension in her shoulders. "This city has shitty infrastructure. Just pray the water main doesn't burst."

I chuckle softly. I want to ask about earlier, about what she was going to say before the lights went out, but something in her posture wards me off. "My ankle feels better already."

"The ice is working, then. Speaking of which..." She gestures toward the window where snow is piling against the glass. "There's no shortage of that for the next few days."

"Silver lining."

"Always looking for the bright side, aren't you?"

There's something almost wistful in her voice. "I'm working on it I guess."

She shakes her head with a smile. "You spend enough time with Eden and you'll be sniffing daisies and smiling a lot more."

The fire pops, and I watch Eliza's profile in the flickering light. She looks younger somehow, softer, without the defensive edge she usually carries.

"You should get out of those wet clothes," she says suddenly, then her cheeks flush. "I mean, you'll catch hypothermia or something. I probably have something that'll fit."

She disappears upstairs, returning with an armload of fabric. "These are my brother-in-law's. Not sure who left them here after a family dinner."

I examine the clothes—flannel pants and a thermal shirt that definitely belong to someone broader than me. "Will I look ridiculous?"

"Probably. But you'll be warm and ridiculous instead of wet and ridiculous."

"Fair point."

Changing clothes with a sprained ankle proves more challenging than expected. Eliza hovers nearby, clearly torn between helping and preserving my dignity. She closes her eyes, and I yank off my wet pants and shirt, trying to cover myself before this woman thinks I'm a total mess.

"I'm fine," I insist, hopping on one foot while trying to pull on the oversized flannel pants. "I suspect you have these because the donkey attacked Koa or Nate."

She giggles—an actual giggle. It's charming, and my delight at the sound causes me to wobble.

Eliza sucks in a breath. "You're going to fall over."

"I'm not going to—" I teeter dangerously, still shirtless.

"For fuck's sake." She steps forward, steadying me with one hand while helping guide my injured foot through the pant leg. The heat of her palm on my skin is enough to make me forget what season we're in. "There. Was that so hard?"

I cannot make a joke about her use of the word *hard*. The borrowed clothes hang loose on my frame, making me look like a kid playing dress-up. Yes, I'll think about how stupid I must appear to distract from my giant boner.

"How do I look?"

"Like a scarecrow," she says, but her smile takes the sting out of it. "A very cute scarecrow."

I pause. "You think I'm cute?"

Eliza breathes in through her nose and stomps over to

the kitchen, emerging with crackers, cheese, a few clementines, and ...

"The soup is cold," she says. "I can heat it on the wood stove and risk burning it, or we can just suck it up and eat it at room temperature. You're the guest, so you choose."

I settle on the couch, propping my ankle on a pillow. I want to talk more about her thinking I'm cute, but my stomach growls loudly, so I say, "Cold soup for the win. Like Gazpacho. Or something."

Eliza smiles, looking like I've passed some sort of test, and busies herself ladling soup, not meeting my eyes.

"Eliza..." I start carefully.

"Dig in," she says and clanks her spoon against mine before taking a bite.

We eat in relative silence, the only sounds being the storm outside and the occasional crackle from the fire. The canned soup is good; I think it's alphabet soup, which I always wanted as a kid, but my mother refused to serve. The accompanying cookies taste even better than they did at the exchange.

"What would you be eating tonight if you had electricity?" I ask, suppressing a moan at the buttery flavor of the cookie.

Eliza shrugs and finishes her soup. "This... but warm." She laughs despite herself, and the sound loosens something in my chest. This feels normal, easy, like we could do this every night and never get tired of it.

"This is nice." I regret the words when she tenses.

"It's just dinner."

"Is it?"

Eliza sets down her spoon, that guarded expression creeping over her features. "Reed—"

"We're snowed in together, eating by candlelight, and you just helped me into borrowed pajamas. You said I'm cute. If this isn't at least a little romantic, I'm seriously misreading the situation."

"You're injured. I'm being practical."

"Are you?"

She stands abruptly, moving toward the window. "I should check on the animals."

"In a blizzard?"

"They might be scared. The wind's really picking up."

"Eliza, you can't go out in this."

"I can't?" Her voice sharpens. "Since when do you decide what I can and can't do?"

I struggle to my feet, wincing as weight hits my ankle. "Since it's dangerous and unnecessary. Your animals have shelter, food, and water. They're fine."

"You don't know that."

"You're willing to risk your safety to avoid talking to me."

"I'm not avoiding anything." She yanks on boots and tugs her scarf in place. Aggressively dressing, if that's possible.

I furrow my brow. "Really? Because every time things get real between us, you find a reason to leave."

"That's not—" She spins to face me, eyes flashing. "You don't understand."

"Then explain it to me."

"I can't... I'm not good at this, Reed. Feelings and relationships and all that emotional bullshit. I take care of animals and run a business and keep my sisters from killing each other. That's what I'm good at."

"You're good at taking care of people, too," I counter. "You took care of me tonight. A few times, actually."

"That's different."

"How?"

She grabs her coat from the hook by the door. "I'm checking on them."

"Not alone, you're not."

"Reed, you can barely walk."

"Then we'll move slowly."

I start toward my coat, and Eliza moves to block me. "This is insane. You'll make your ankle worse."

"And you'll freeze to death out there."

"I've been taking care of myself for years."

"That doesn't mean you have to."

We're standing close now, close enough that I can see the fear beneath her anger. I can see her pulse thrum in her neck, the shine on her lips where she licks them with her tongue. She's not worried about the goats. She's worried about what happens if we stay here together, in this warm, candlelit space where pretending we're just friends becomes impossible.

"Give me the coat," I say, reaching for the garment in her hands.

"No." She pulls it closer to her chest.

"Eliza."

"Reed."

Somehow we're both holding her scarf now, each of us pulling gently in opposite directions like we're children fighting over a toy. But there's nothing childish about the way she's looking at me or the way my heart is hammering against my ribs.

"You can't keep running," I whisper.

"Watch me," she says, but her voice wavers.

The scarf stretches between us, soft wool connecting us across two feet of charged air. Outside, the wind howls, and inside, something else entirely builds to a storm. I smile, appreciating the perfection of her last name. I let go of my end of the scarf.

19

———

REED

Eliza stumbles slightly from the sudden release of tension.

"Fine," I breathe. "Go check on your animals."

She blinks, clearly surprised by my capitulation. "I... fine. Good."

She wraps the scarf around her neck and heads for the door, but I'm already reaching for my coat.

"What are you doing?" she asks.

"Coming with you."

"Reed, your ankle—"

"Will be fine for a short walk." I pull on my jacket, ignoring the way she stares at me. "Besides, someone needs to make sure you don't blow away in this wind."

"I told you I can take care of myself."

"Trust me, I know."

She opens her mouth to argue, then seems to think better of it. "If you fall and hurt yourself worse, I'm leaving you in a snowbank."

"Deal."

The blizzard hits us like a physical force the moment we step outside. Snow drives horizontally across the yard, and the wind is loud enough that we have to shout to hear each other. Eliza takes my arm—whether to steady me or herself, I'm not sure—and we trudge toward the barn.

Inside, it's blissfully quiet and warm. The animals look up at our entrance but seem completely unbothered by the storm. Chiron stands in his stall, methodically working through a pile of hay, while the goats huddle together in their pen like furry conspirators.

"Great," Eliza says, brushing snow from her jacket. "Completely fine."

I watch her move through the barn, checking water levels and adjusting blankets. "They're lucky to have you."

"They're easy. Animals make sense. Feed them, keep them warm, give them space when they need it." She pauses at Persephone's stall. "No hidden agendas or complicated emotions."

"Is that what you think I have? Hidden agendas?"

Eliza leans against the stall door, suddenly looking exhausted. "I don't know what you have, Reed. That's the problem."

I move closer, my ankle protesting. "Want to know what I'm really afraid of?"

She glances up, wary. "What?"

"That I'm going to fail. That this whole tree business is just an expensive way to prove my father right." I settle onto a hay bale, stretching my injured leg. "That I'll end up in his office, wearing a suit and pretending to care about profit margins and market penetration."

"That's not going to happen."

"How do you know?"

"You care too much about your trees to give up on them." Eliza sits across from me. "And you're too stubborn to let your father win."

"I've been letting him win my whole life." The words taste bitter. "Every family dinner when I bit my tongue instead of arguing. Every time he dismissed my interests as phases. Even at the presentation, I stood there while he humiliated me."

"You didn't stand there. You kept your cool."

"Only because I didn't want to make a scene."

Eliza looks at her hands. "There's strength in choosing your battles."

"You'd know. You're always strong."

The words hang between us in the warm air, mixing with the sounds of animals settling for the night. Chiron munches contentedly on his hay, occasionally glancing our way like he's eavesdropping.

"My mother used to tell me I was her favorite," Eliza says suddenly. "Every time she showed up after being gone for weeks or months, she'd say I was the only one who understood her. That we had a special connection."

I wait, sensing there's more.

"I believed her. Every single time. Even when Eden was crying because Mom missed her school play, or when Eila got in trouble because no one was there to sign her permission slips." Eliza's voice gets quieter. "I thought being her favorite meant something. That it made me special."

"Eliza..."

"But it didn't. She left anyway, and when she came

back, she'd tell one of my sisters the exact same thing." Eliza looks up at me. "So when you say I'm strong, that you want me, part of me wonders what you'll say to the next woman when you get tired of this one."

The comparison stings deep. "I'm not your mother."

"Logically, I know that. But knowing something and feeling it are different things."

I stand up, ignoring the twinge in my ankle, and sit beside her on the hay bale. "What would help you feel it?"

"I don't know. Maybe therapy? My sisters have been going, and they seem... better. Less likely to set things on fire when they're upset."

"That sounds like a good idea."

"For them. I don't know if it would work for me."

"Why not?"

Eliza shrugs. "Admitting I need help feels like admitting I'm broken."

"Or it feels like admitting you're human." I bump her shoulder gently. "Tell you what... I'll go to therapy if you do."

"That's ridiculous."

"Is it? We could make it a competition. See who makes the most progress."

Despite herself, Eliza smiles. "You want to turn mental health into a contest?"

"I want to turn it into something you can win. You're competitive as hell, and if there's a chance you can beat me at something, you'll try."

"You're not wrong." She considers this. "Instead of spending fifteen thousand on tree damage, we'll spend it on therapy bills."

"An excellent investment."

"Definitely." Eliza turns to face me more fully. "But I'm warning you now—I'm going to win this mental health challenge."

"Bring it on, Storm."

Her name fits her perfectly—unpredictable, powerful, impossible to ignore. And when she looks at me like she is now, with something soft and hopeful in her eyes, I feel like I'm standing in the eye of the hurricane.

"Reed?" she says quietly.

"Yeah?"

"I'm scared."

"Of what?"

"Of how much I want this. Want you." She takes a shaky breath. "Of how much it's going to hurt when you figure out I'm not worth the trouble."

"Eliza." I cup her face in my hands. "You are worth every bit of trouble. You're worth fighting for, worth waiting for, worth whatever chaos comes with loving you."

"Loving me?"

The words slipped out, but I don't take them back. "Yeah. Loving you. I'm setting that as a goal."

Her eyes search my face like she's looking for signs of deception. Whatever she sees must satisfy her, because she leans forward and kisses me.

It's soft at first, tentative, like she's not entirely sure this is real. But when I kiss her back, when I pull her closer and she makes this small sound of surprise and pleasure, everything changes.

This isn't the almost-kiss from the kitchen or the cheek kiss outside Esther's house. This is Eliza deciding to trust me, to stop running, to let herself want something good.

Her hands fist in my borrowed flannel shirt as she deepens the kiss, and I can taste the sweetness of the cookies we shared earlier. She's warm and alive and here, and for the first time in weeks, I'm not worried about what comes next.

When we break apart, we're both breathing hard.

"Wow," Eliza says.

"Yeah. Wow."

She grins that mischievous expression I've learned to love and fear in equal measure. "So... now what?"

"Now..." I trace my thumb along her cheekbone. "I'd really like to make you feel good."

Her breath catches. "Reed..."

"Only if you want. No pressure, no expectations. I just..." I search for words. "I want to touch you. I want to know what you sound like when you're not holding back."

"We don't have... I mean, we're in a barn."

"You've never wanted to get a little naughty out here?" I arch a brow and lean a little closer, half because of my ankle and half because I need to feel her against more of my body.

Understanding dawns in her eyes, followed immediately by want. "Oh."

"Is that a yes?"

Instead of answering, she kisses me again, harder this time, with an urgency that makes my head spin. Her hands slide under my shirt, fingernails scraping lightly against my chest, and I groan against her mouth.

"Yes," she breathes. "Definitely yes."

I ease her onto the hay, mindful of the scratchy surface, kissing my way down her neck while she arches beneath me.

"Wait." She spins out from beneath my body and yanks a blanket from where it's draped on a beam. "The hay is poky." She smooths out the blanket as I watch and then nestles her body into the makeshift nest. "Okay, continue."

I huff a laugh at her enthusiasm, but hurry to pick up where I stopped. I shove her layers out of the way, licking her exposed skin. She smells like vanilla and wood smoke and something uniquely her I want to memorize.

"Tell me what you like," I murmur against her collarbone.

"I don't know. I mean, I know what I like when I'm alone, but with someone else..." She sounds breathless, uncertain.

I meet her eye, aware that she is telling me her previous partners haven't prioritized her. The thought overwhelms me when all I can think about is her—her pleasure, her needs, her strong and capable body. I swallow a growl. "We'll figure it out together."

I take my time, despite the throb in my borrowed pants, learning the sensitive spot just below her ear that makes her gasp. She shivers when I kiss the hollow of her throat. When I reach for the hem of her sweater, she helps me pull it over her head, revealing a simple cotton bra that somehow looks incredibly sexy in the golden barn light.

She trembles briefly, and I nestle closer to her, hoping to lend her my heat. "You're beautiful."

"I'm practical," she says, but she's smiling.

"You're beautiful *and* practical. And absolutely perfect."

I kiss my way across her collarbone, down to the soft swell of her breasts, taking my time while she runs her fingers through my hair. It feels so good to be with her this way, tinkering with her magnificent body, invited to explore and touch and sip as much as I want.

And I want. I want very badly.

When I reach for the band of her bra, she nods, and I free her breasts to the chilly air.

"Reed," she breathes when I take one nipple into my mouth, and the sound goes straight to my cock.

I lavish attention on her breasts while working her jeans open, taking cues from the sounds she makes and the way her hips move beneath me. When I slide my hand inside her panties, she's already wet.

"God, Eliza," I murmur against her skin. "You feel incredible. How are you real?" This smart, sassy woman who challenges me in every way is finally bared beneath me, and her body is responding.

To *me*.

She pulls my head up for another kiss, this one desperate and demanding. I stroke her slowly at first, delighting in each hitch of her breath, each spasm of her abs.

"You're so wet," I murmur into her mouth, matching the thrusting of my finger inside her with the stroke of my tongue inside her mouth. All the energy of the past few weeks, all the tension about my business and my budding infatuation with this tornado of a woman culminate in the pulsing, gasping, shuddering experience here in a haystack.

When Eliza groans and stutters out my name, I pick up the pace and increase the pressure of my thumb above her folds, watching her face release as she gets closer to the edge.

"I'm going to..." she gasps.

"Let go," I tell her. "I've got you."

When she comes, it's with a soft cry that echoes through the barn, her body tensing and then melting beneath my touch. I work her through it, kissing her neck and whispering how amazing she is until the aftershocks fade.

As she calms, I withdraw my hand, the scent of her on my fingers overwhelming. My cock throbs in my pants, and I lick my fingertips, tasting the spiced salt of Eliza's arousal.

"That was..." She blinks at me, dazed and satisfied.

"Okay?"

"Beyond amazing." She grins, then her expression turns predatory. "My turn."

"Eliza, you don't have to—"

"I want to." She pushes me onto the rustling nest of hay, straddling my hips with a confidence that makes my cock twitch. "I want to touch you." The taste of her lingers on my tongue, and I'm half-drunk with lust. I'm not about to deny her anything.

When she reaches for the waistband of my pants, I lift my hips to help her. The flannel slides down easily, taking my boxers with it, and suddenly I'm exposed to the gusty barn air and Eliza's appreciative gaze.

"Well, hello there," she says with a smirk that nearly undoes me.

"Eliza..." I have serious concerns that my erection will

fade in the drafty breeze, but there she is above me. There's the scent of her everywhere. Lusty and thick and... oh, she's smiling at my dick.

"Shh." She wraps her hand around my length, testing the weight and feel of me. "Let me take care of you."

Her grip is dry at first, but so warm and firm. A groan escapes my lips, and my hips jut involuntarily even as she frowns. "Hmm," she says, releasing me. My dick falls against my stomach with a *thwap,* and I open my eyes to see her opening a small jar.

"Udder balm?" I squint, certain I'm hallucinating.

She scoops out a dab and rubs her palms together, making a facial expression that's pure filth. "It's basically expensive hand lotion." She warms her hands together, still sitting astride my hips with her tits out, toned stomach flexing with her movements. "Trust me."

When she wraps her newly slick hand around me, all coherent thought abandons my brain. The ointment provides perfect glide, and Eliza's touch is confident and sure as she finds a rhythm that has me gripping the hay beneath us.

"You like this?" she asks, watching my face.

"God, yes. Fuck, nothing has ever been this hot. Ever. Fuck, Eliza."

She adjusts her grip, thumb swiping over the head of my cock in a way that makes my hips buck. "What about this?"

"Eliza, if you keep doing that, I'm going to..."

"Good." She leans down to kiss me while maintaining that perfect rhythm. "I want to watch you come."

The combination of her hand on my shaft and her mouth on mine is more than I can handle. When the orgasm hits, it's with an intensity that leaves me gasping her name and clutching at her shoulders.

She works me through it until I'm boneless and spent, then reaches for a rag to wipe her hands.

"Good?" she asks, settling beside me on the blanket. The air smells like sex and barn and a little like soup. It's absolutely intoxicating.

"Ungh, beyond amazing." I echo her words and pull her close, marveling at how perfectly she fits against my side. "You're incredible."

"*We're* incredible," she corrects, and I can hear the smile in her voice.

Outside, the storm continues to rage, but here in the barn with Eliza in my arms and snoring animals nearby, everything feels exactly as it should be.

"So," Eliza says, tracing patterns on my chest. "What happens now?"

"We go to the house, and I hold you on that uncomfortable couch until we fall asleep."

She giggles. "We can try my bed, I think." She pauses. "And tomorrow?"

"Tomorrow, we see if the roads are clear enough for me to take you shopping for a dress for the Yule Gala."

She lifts her head to look at me. "You still want me to go with you?"

"Eliza, I want you with me everywhere."

She grins, that radiant smile that first caught my attention in the permit office. "Okay then. But I'd rather wear pants."

"Whatever you wish, Storm."

As if on cue, Chiron lets out a contented bray, and we both start laughing.

20

———————

ELIZA

I wake up to the weight of Reed's arm across my waist. For a moment, I'm disoriented—this is my bed, my room, but there's a warm male body pressed against my back and the smell of hay clinging to both of us.

Then I remember. The storm, the barn, Reed's hands all over me and the way he looked at me like I was something precious instead of damaged.

Reed shifts, his breath warm against my neck. "Morning," he murmurs, voice thick with sleep.

"Morning." I turn in his arms, staring at his disheveled hair and the stubble shadowing his jaw. In the daylight, last night feels almost surreal. "How's your ankle?"

"Better." He flexes his foot experimentally. "Sore, but I think I can put weight on it."

"Good." I study his face, looking for signs of regret or awkwardness, but all I see is the same warmth from last night. "So..."

"So." He smiles, and it's so real, so happy I almost

don't know what to do about it. This man is happy to wake up beside me.

We stare at each other for a moment, and I feel the familiar urge to bolt, to make some excuse about morning chores and disappear before things get complicated. But Reed brushes the hair from my face, and the gesture is so gentle I stay put.

"I want to keep doing this," he says quietly. "Not just the sex stuff, though that was incredible. But this. Us. Whatever we're building here."

Relief floods through me at his directness. "Me too. But we have to be really clear about everything. I'm not used to this."

"No games," he says. "Just honesty."

I trace a finger along his torso, remembering how I kissed him there last night. A bunch of times. I hum happily. "Then honestly... I need to go check on the animals."

Reed nods, but when he tries to sit up, he winces. "Shit. I can't tell if I messed up my body falling on the ice or hauling bales of hay with you." He flexes and rotates his wrists. "No wonder you're so buff."

I huff but appreciate that he notices things I'm proud of about myself. Like my muscles. "Stay here," I tell him, already pulling on clothes. "Rest your ankle. I'll be quick."

"Eliza—"

"You helped me yesterday when you could barely walk. Let me take care of you for once."

He opens his mouth to argue, then seems to think better of it. "Fine, but if you're not back in twenty minutes, I'm coming after you."

"Deal."

I pull on boots and my coat, then step outside into a world transformed by snow. Everything is white and pristine, the storm having dumped at least eight inches overnight. My truck is buried, but I can see tire tracks in the road where the plows have been through.

The animals are fine—their water bowls didn't even freeze, probably thanks to the heat Reed and I generated in the barn last night. I smile, remembering how good everything felt with him, how he didn't rush me, but I came fast and hard for him, anyway.

Chiron interrupts my daydream with an accusatory bray—apparently I'm late with the breakfast pellets—but the goats seem content with their warm barn and full hay nets.

"Sorry, guys," I tell them as I distribute fresh water and morning grain. "I was... occupied."

Ursula gives me a look that suggests she knows exactly what I was occupied with, which is ridiculous, because she's a goat. But there's definitely judgment in those yellow eyes.

I'm back at the house in fifteen minutes, stomping snow off my boots before heading upstairs. I can hear the shower running, which means Reed ignored my advice to rest.

"Stubborn ass," I mutter, but I'm smiling.

I find him in my tiny bathroom, struggling to wash his hair while keeping weight off his injured ankle. Steam fogs the mirror, and through the clear shower curtain, I can see the lean lines of his body, the way water runs down his chest and over the flat plane of his stomach.

"Need help?" I ask.

Reed startles, nearly losing his balance. "I thought you were outside."

"I was. Animals are fed and watered." I pull off my clothes. "Scoot over."

"Eliza, you don't have to—"

"Reed, shut up and let me help you."

He steps aside to make room as I climb into the small shower stall. The space is cramped with both of us in here, but I don't mind being pressed against his warm, wet body.

"Turn around," I tell him, reaching for the honey and goat milk soap I made with Eden. "Let me wash your back."

He obeys, and I work the soap into a rich lather, massaging his shoulders while he leans against me. His skin is smoother than I expected, and I take my time, enjoying the intimacy of the simple act.

"This is nice," he mumbles.

"Mmm." I rinse the soap from him, then work on his lower back, kneading the tension and hopefully easing the soreness he mentioned.

When my soapy hands reach around to slide down his chest, Reed's breathing changes. When they drift lower, to his stomach and then below, he groans and braces against the shower wall.

"Eliza..."

"What?" I wrap my hand around his rapidly hardening cock, stroking slowly. "Problem?"

"The opposite of a problem." He groans as I tighten my grip, and I love how it feels to give him pleasure. This is all so new to me, enjoying myself with a man. I really like it. And that terrifies me, but it's hard to dwell on that as I have him here with me, moaning in response to my movements.

I work him with the same attention to detail I gave his muscles, learning what pressure and rhythm make his breath catch, what movements have him pushing into my grip. The soap provides a better glide than the udder ointment, and soon he's panting my name and thrusting helplessly into my fist as I press my boobs into his back.

I want to see his face when he comes, so I slide around him and gasp at what I see. Reed is a man undone, neck muscles taut, eyes squeezed shut, mouth hanging open. I love knowing I brought him here, disheveled him, found what he likes.

When he comes, it's with a broken cry that echoes off the bathroom tiles, his release mixing with the warm water on my wrist and washing down the drain.

"Jesus," he gasps, folding me in his arms. "That was…"

"Thorough hygiene?"

"Fucking amazing hygiene."

He kisses me hard and grateful, and I can taste the promise of more mornings like this in the press of his lips.

We finish showering without further incident, though Reed insists on returning the favor by washing my hair with the same careful attention I gave his, including a thorough rub down my center and a soaped-up clit that makes me scream. By the time we exhaust the hot water, he's moving much better on his ankle, and my legs are jelly.

"Roads should be clear enough," he says, getting dressed in his clothes from yesterday. "I should head to work, let you get back to your routine."

"Okay." I try to keep the disappointment out of my voice. I know he has to leave, know we both have responsibilities, but part of me wants to keep him in this snow-globe version of my life where nothing exists except us and the animals.

"I want to see you again," he adds quickly. "Soon. Maybe tonight? We could grab dinner, talk about the Yule Gala."

"I'd like that."

He kisses me goodbye at the front door, a soft, lingering press that makes me want to drag him upstairs. Instead, I watch from the window as he carefully navigates his way to his car, brushing snow off the windshield before climbing inside.

I'm still watching his taillights disappear down the road when my phone buzzes with a text message. Thinking it's Reed, using voice text to send something cute, I pull my phone out immediately. But it's not him.

The number isn't in my contacts, though I recognize it immediately.

Hi sweetheart! It's Mom. Hope this is still your number! I have the most wonderful news to share with you girls. I'm coming home for the holidays! I've found the perfect business opportunity for us to work on together. I know how much you've always wanted to expand your little animal service, and I think I've found the solution. Can't wait to see my successful daughters! We have so much to catch up on. Love and kisses, Mom

I READ the message three times, my good mood evaporating more with each pass. The casual endearments, the fake enthusiasm, the assumption I've been waiting for her help with my "little animal service."

Most telling of all: "my successful daughters." Emma Storm only shows up when she thinks there's something in it for her. I remember last year she tried to wreck Eden's beekeeping business and horn in on the beeswax products Eden's been selling. The last thing I need is my mother interfering with my goats, especially when I'm in precarious financial straits with MUNCH.

I sink onto my couch, already missing Reed sitting here with me, and stare at the text until the words blur together. Just when everything was starting to feel possible—Reed, the therapy plan, the tentative hope that maybe I could trust someone—my mother decides to reappear with whatever scheme she's cooked up this time.

Outside, the snow continues to fall, and for the first time since the storm started, I feel truly cold.

21

REED

I'M LIMPING AROUND MY GREENHOUSE LIKE SOME KIND OF mad scientist-pirate, alternating between euphoric grins at the memory of Eliza's hands on my body and crushing anxiety about the spreadsheet on my tablet showing exactly how fucked I am financially.

Three weeks. That's how much operating capital I have left before I'll be forced to shut down Urban Forest Solutions and crawl to my father's office with my tail between my legs. The presentation at Bramblewood was supposed to generate interest, but it generated exactly zero investment inquiries and one very public humiliation.

I am in the midst of the December holiday season with no mass-produced product and barely a spare proto-type. These tiny trees are perfect—healthy, symmetrical, exactly what I envisioned when I started this whole venture. But perfect doesn't matter if no one's willing to fund their production. At least the Bramblewood folks still want my trees as centerpieces for the gala. I should head over there at some point and check on the trees... make sure no more wildlife got loose in the manor or something.

I smile again, thinking of my night with Eliza. All of this is too much, but somehow, it feels approachable, knowing a feisty goatherd is on my side.

"Yo, Reed!" Paolo's voice echoes through the greenhouse as he pushes through the door. "Can I ask you a big favor?"

"Maybe," I tease, grateful for the distraction. "What are you doing here?"

"Heading to my cousin's for Immaculate Conception stuff and thought I'd ask if I could snag one of your trees. My abuela's been asking about my 'so-called friends', and I figured..." He gestures around the lab with a grin.

I wave an arm toward the display area. "Take your pick."

Paolo examines the trees with exaggerated seriousness before selecting a particularly full specimen. "This one's calling to me. Very Feng Shui."

"That'll be—"

"Don't even think about charging me," Paolo interrupts. "Consider it payment for all the times I've had to listen to you obsess over pH levels."

I watch him cradle the small tree carefully, and something twists in my chest. In a few weeks, I'll be giving all these trees away or watching them die as I pack this place.

"So," Paolo says, settling the tree on his hip, "how are things with the goat lady? You've been suspiciously happy, despite your impending financial doom."

Heat creeps through my neck. "We're… we've made some progress."

"Progress?" Paolo's eyebrows shoot up. "That's the most euphemistic way I've ever heard someone describe getting laid."

"It's not just that," I protest, though my face is probably burning red. "We talked. Really talked. About real things."

"Aw, look at you being all emotionally mature." Paolo grins. "I'm proud of you, man. Even if your business implodes, at least you won't be alone."

The reminder of my failing business makes my stomach clench, but Paolo's genuine happiness for me softens the blow. "Thanks. I think."

"Hey, things could turn around. You never know." Paolo heads toward the door with his tree. "Enjoy the holidays, Reed. And don't marry your farmer girlfriend until I get back."

"She's not my girlfriend—" But Paolo's already gone, leaving me alone with the echo of his laughter and the space where the tree used to be.

I stare at the gap in my lineup, the way the other trees seem to lean slightly toward the absence. In a few weeks, this entire greenhouse will look like that—empty spaces where my dreams used to be.

My tablet buzzes with an email notification, probably another rejection or my landlord asking about next month's rent. I'm tempted to ignore it, but procrastination won't pay my bills.

The sender's domain name makes me blink twice: North Shore Capital.

I squint at the screen, my insides fluttering with hope I thought was squashed.

Mr. Nicholas,

I apologize for the delayed invitation to your presentation at Bramblewood Manor. I was traveling and have only recently had the opportunity to review the materials you provided.

Your hydroponic forestry concept is intriguing, and I'd like to discuss potential investment opportunities. I'll be attending the Yule Gala at Bramblewood this Friday and would appreciate the chance to speak with you about your projections in more detail.

JENNIFER MARTINEZ, senior partner at an investment group, has asked me for forecasts and sales models. With no mention of my father, his company, or anything related to Nicholas Industries. She's... interested in my work.

I read the email three times before it sinks in. An investor. An actual investor who wants to see projections and marketing strategies and scaling scenarios.

Holy shit.

I plunge into full panic mode, my mind racing through everything I need to prepare. Financial forecasts, marketing plans, production timelines—none of which I have in the format a serious investor would expect. I grab my laptop and pull up spreadsheets, my fingers flying over the keyboard.

Five hundred units. A thousand. Twenty-five hundred. The numbers swim in front of my eyes as I try to calculate everything from raw materials to shipping costs to labor requirements. This is exactly the kind of detailed analysis I should have prepared weeks ago, but I was too focused on a sales pitch for my science to think about the business side.

My phone buzzes. Then again. I glance at it briefly—Eliza's name on the screen—but I'm deep in a calculation about nutrient solution costs and can't break concentration. I'll call her once I get this under control.

The forecasting takes hours. By the time I look up, it's completely dark outside, and my phone is showing multiple missed calls and texts. My mother called twice, probably to lecture me about missing the ballet and avoiding my father's job offer. But most of the missed notifications are from Eliza.

I scroll through her texts:

Hey, how's the ankle?

Call me when you get this

Really need to talk to you

Reed? Everything okay?

I guess you're busy. Call me tonight if you can

THE LAST MESSAGE was sent three hours ago. I should call her back, but I'm in the zone now, bar charts and pivot tables sprouting like weeds. I'm finally making real progress on the business materials, and I can't afford to lose momentum.

My phone rings again—my mother's number this time. I answer on speaker, barely paying attention.

"Reed, darling, where have you been?" Her voice carries that particular tone of disappointment I've been hearing since childhood. "You already missed the Nutcracker, and your father is furious about your continued avoidance of his very generous job offer."

"I'm working, Mom."

"Working on what? That little tree thing? Reed, you need to be practical. Your father has been more than patient, but you need to prepare for your arrival at the company."

"I'm not taking the job."

"Don't be ridiculous. You can't live off your agricultural nonsense. Why pass up a sure paycheck?"

The words sting because she's not entirely wrong. If this investor meeting doesn't work out, I'll be exactly where my parents predicted—broke, failed, and crawling to Nicholas Industries.

"I have to go," I say.

"Reed, we need to discuss—"

I hang up and switch my phone to silent. Then, thinking better of it, I power it off completely. Eliza will understand that I'm working. She runs her own business; she knows how consuming that can be.

Right now, I need to focus. Jennifer Martinez is my last chance to save Urban Forest Solutions, and I'll be damned if I'm going to blow it this time.

I scratch out a rough calendar on my whiteboard. The gala is on Friday, four days away. Four days to create a presentation that could save everything I've worked for. A presentation that's effortlessly cool while also impactful.

Four days to prove my father was wrong about me. To prove to Eliza and maybe even myself that my idealistic vision matters.

22

ELIZA

By 8:00 pm, I've called Reed three times and sent four texts with no response. I feel like some sort of teenage drama queen. I'm not sure I've ever reached out to someone this many times in one day. This morning feels like a fever dream—the intimacy in the shower, his promise to see me tonight, the way he kissed me goodbye and meant it.

Maybe he got absorbed in his work. Reed's the type to lose track of time when he's focused on his trees. I tell myself this is normal, that entrepreneurs get tunnel vision, that I'm overreacting.

But the damaged part of my brain keeps whispering that rich boys always bail once they get what they want.

My phone buzzes, and I grab it eagerly, hoping to see Reed's name. Instead, it's another text from my mother.

Can't wait to see my successful girls! I have so many exciting opportunities to share. What's your address, sweetie? I want to surprise you!

I stare at the message, my stomach clenching. Emma wanting my address is never good news. She only shows up when she needs something, and the fact that she's being coy about it means whatever she's planning is big.

I power off my phone and shove it in a drawer. If Reed wants to ignore me, fine. If my mother wants to play games, she can do it without me.

I throw myself into evening chores with more aggression than necessary, mucking stalls and refilling water troughs as if I'm being watched by someone other than my animals. Chiron stares with what might be concern, or maybe judgment. Hard to tell with donkeys.

For dinner, I eat three cookies from the batch Reed and I made together, standing at my kitchen counter in the dark. If I turn my phone on, I might have a call from Reed, but I also might not and so I just keep eating cookies until my stomach hurts. The butter and vanilla taste like yesterday's happiness, before everything got complicated.

I'M ankle-deep in morning goat manure, trying to work out my frustration through physical labor, when I hear a car door slam in my driveway. My heart leaps—maybe Reed came to explain himself.

But when I look up, it's not Reed's hybrid. It's a silver taxi, and stepping out of it with a giant suitcase and an armload of boxes labeled "Diamond Elite Wellness Journey" is Emma Storm.

My mother looks exactly the same as she did six months ago when she tried to convince Eden to sell her beeswax products through some sketchy multilevel marketing scheme. Blonde hair in a perfect blowout, expensive-looking coat, and that smile that never quite reaches her eyes.

"Eliza, sweetheart!" she calls, waving like we're old friends instead of a mother and daughter who haven't spoken since June. "Surprise!"

I set down my pitchfork and walk toward her, hyper-aware of the manure on my boots and the contrast between her polished appearance and my work clothes. "How did you find me?"

Emma laughs as the taxi bumps down my lane. Mom's giggle is the tinkling sound she makes when she's pleased with her own cleverness. "Property records, darling. Amazing what you can find online these days. I tried calling your sisters, but they seem to have changed their numbers." Her smile falters. "Can you imagine?"

I don't need to imagine. In fact, I know exactly why my sisters stopped taking her calls. The last time my mother showed up, she kicked over Eden's beehives and melted her stockpile of wax. Everyone but me did a good job setting boundaries.

"What are you doing here, Emma?"

"Emma?" She presses a hand to her chest in mock hurt. "I'm your mother, darling. I'm here because I have the most incredible opportunity to share with you." She sweeps a Vanna-White-style wrist, gesturing at the product boxes lined on my lane.

I frown, but resist stabbing them with my pitchfork.

"Come on," Mom says, grabbing her suitcase. "Let's get inside, so I can tell you all about Diamond Elite Wellness Journey. You're going to love this."

I don't move. "You can't just show up here unannounced."

"Of course I can. I'm your mother." Emma looks around my property with an expression somewhere between amusement and pity. "This is charming, Eliza. Very rustic. Like a hobby farm."

The casual insult hits exactly where she intended. "This is my business."

"Of course it is, sweetie." She pats my arm. "It's adorable, but wait until you hear about the income potential with Diamond Elite. We're talking about real money here."

She pushes past me toward the house, and I follow, feeling like a child again. This is how it always goes with Emma—she sweeps in, takes control, and suddenly I'm reacting instead of acting.

Inside, she sets down her suitcase and immediately starts commenting on everything. "Oh, this is cozy. Very... minimalist. Are you going for that shabby-chic look on purpose?"

I scowl, noting the difference between her response and my sisters, who noticed my decorations, and Reed, who seemed charmed by my candles. "It's just how I live."

"Well, that's about to change." Emma opens one of her boxes and pulls out glossy brochures and sample products. "Diamond Elite Wellness Journey is going to revolutionize how we think about health and financial freedom. And you, my dear daughter, are going to be one of my first distributors."

"I'm not interested in—"

"Don't be silly. You've always been my entrepreneur." She spreads brochures across my coffee table, marking her territory. "This is exactly what you need to take your little animal service to the next level."

I need something to do with my hands to avoid wringing her neck, so I turn on my phone. It starts buzzing immediately with missed messages. Emma's eyes immediately dart toward the sound.

"Aren't you going to check that? It might be important."

I glance down, hoping it's one of my sisters texting back about Emma's arrival. Instead, it's Reed.

> Sorry for disappearing yesterday. Got caught up in a work emergency, but that's no excuse. On my way over with apology cocoa and possibly mistletoe for next year's tree repertoire. Hope that's okay.

Relief floods through me, followed immediately by panic. Reed cannot meet my mother. Not like this, not when she's in full pyramid scheme mode, and I'm barely keeping my head above water.

"Who's that?" Emma asks, noting my expression. "You're smiling. Is it a boy?"

"It's nobody."

But Emma's already moving closer, trying to read over my shoulder. "Reed Nicholas? As in Nicholas Industries?"

Shit. "How do you know about Nicholas Industries?"

Emma's face lights up and I can practically see her

spinning plans. "Darling, everyone in Pittsburgh knows about Nicholas Industries. They're major developers, big money." She grabs my arm. "Are you dating Charles Nicholas's son?"

I shake my head. She cannot have this. Not Reed. "It's complicated."

"Complicated how? Eliza, this is incredible. Do you know what this means for Diamond Elite? If we could get Nicholas Industries to invest, or even just endorse our line—"

"Stop." I pull my arm away. "It's not like that."

"Not like what? Sweetie, opportunity doesn't knock twice. If you're involved with someone from one of Pittsburgh's most prominent families—"

"Reed isn't like that. And neither am I."

Emma stares at me like I've grown a second head. "Not like what? Ambitious? Smart enough to leverage your connections?"

"Manipulative."

The word hangs between us, sharp and cutting. Emma's smile falters for the first time since she arrived.

"That's a horrible thing to say to your mother."

"Is it? You showed up here planning to use me for something, and now you want to use my relationship, too."

"I want to help you succeed."

"By selling potions and oils to my friends? By turning my boyfriend into a business contact?" I shake my head. "That's not help, Emma. That's using people."

For a moment, Emma looks genuinely hurt. Then her expression hardens into something more familiar—the look she gets when people don't play along with her schemes. The look she'd give when we couldn't quite manage to keep social services away when we were living in a car between evictions, for instance.

"Fine," she says. "I can see you're not in the right headspace to discuss this rationally. I'll just stay in my room until you come around."

"You'll what?"

"My room, silly. I'm sure there's more than one in this old farmhouse. I don't have anywhere else to go, and we're family." She settles onto my couch like she's planning to nest. "It'll be fun. Like a girls' trip."

"Emma, you can't just—"

"I'm your mother, Eliza." For just a second, her mask slips, and I see something vulnerable underneath. "Please."

The *please* gets me, just like it always does. Despite everything, despite knowing better, part of me wants to be the daughter who can fix things for her.

But I think about Reed, about the therapy promise we made, about the boundaries my sisters have learned to set.

"Okay," I say finally. "You can stay, but there are rules."

Emma brightens. "Of course."

"No pyramid schemes in my house. No using my relationships for business contacts. And this is temporary— one week, maximum."

"One week?" Emma's smile falters. "Sweetie, it's the holidays. That's hardly enough time to—"

"One week, or you can find somewhere else to stay."

We stare at each other for a long moment. Finally, Emma nods. "Fine. One week."

I grab my phone and start texting:

STORM CLOUD GROUP CHAT

EMERGENCY. Mom is here with MLM boxes and needs a place to stay. Send help.

THEN I REPLY TO REED.

Rain check on cocoa? Family emergency. Will explain later.

As I hit send, I catch Emma watching me with that calculating expression I know all too well. One week feels like a lifetime.

I have a sinking feeling even that might be too long.

23

____

REED

Eliza's rain check text flashes on my phone screen, worry nagging at me. *Family emergency* could mean anything, but combined with her frantic messages yesterday, my gut tells me something's wrong.

I should respect her boundaries, give her space to handle whatever's happening. That's what a mature, emotionally intelligent boyfriend would do.

But I also sort of bailed after asking her to dinner, and we had a barn-chat about both of us needing therapy for our emotional wounds, so I pull into her driveway with two thermoses of cocoa and a growing certainty she needs backup.

Through Eliza's front window, I can see two figures having an intense conversation. When I knock, Eliza opens the door, looking harried and trapped.

"Reed? I told you—"

"Who's this handsome young man?" interrupts a voice from behind her.

The woman who appears is clearly related to Eliza—

same stature, similar facial features—but everything else is different. Where Eliza is practical and authentic, this woman is coiffed and artificial, an avatar of what a successful person should look like.

"Reed Nicholas," I say, extending my hand. "You must be Eliza's mother."

"Emma Storm." Her grip is firm, assessing. "And yes, I'm Eliza's mother, though she's been keeping you quite the secret." Her smile sharpens. "She said your father is Charles Nicholas?"

"Reed's not—" Eliza starts, but Emma steamrolls right over her.

"I was just telling Eliza about an incredible business opportunity, and this is perfect timing. Would you like to hear about Diamond Elite Wellness Journey?"

I glance at Eliza, who's gone pale and looks like she wants to disappear into the floorboards. There's something familiar about her expression—the same trapped, diminished look I get when my father starts one of his lectures about my life choices.

"I'd be happy to listen," I say carefully, not wanting anything to do with a woman who immediately associates me with my father.

Emma's face lights up. "Wonderful! Let me get my materials."

She bustles toward the coffee table, which is covered in glossy brochures and product samples. Eliza catches my arm.

"You don't have to..."

"It's fine," I murmur. "I've got this." Eliza's eyes are wet, like she's near tears, and I squeeze her arm, trying to convey that I'm here for her, that I'm on to her mother's act. Only when I smile and tug her hand does she agree to join me on the sofa.

For the next ten minutes, Emma delivers what I recognize as a scripted presentation about supplements, financial freedom, and "being your own boss." She uses terms like "ground floor opportunity" and "exponential growth potential" while showing me income charts that would make any scientist cringe.

I take frantic mental notes on what not to do in my pitch in a few days, though something tells me I could appear more genuine than this without much effort.

"So," Emma concludes with a dazzling smile, "are you ready to join the Diamond Elite family?"

"It sounds interesting," I say diplomatically. "But I'd need to see some additional information first."

"Of course! What would you like to know?"

"Could you provide documentation of the company's compensation structure? Specifically, what percentage of distributors achieve the income levels shown in these charts?"

Emma's smile falters. "Well, individual results vary, but the potential is unlimited for people willing to work hard."

"I understand, but I need actual data. Success rates, average earnings, that sort of thing." I keep my tone pleasant but persistent, thinking of the specific data points I'm being asked to present on Friday. "I actually have a PhD in biochemistry, so I'm curious about the scientific evidence supporting your product claims as well."

"Evidence?" Emma looks like I've asked her to perform surgery.

"Yes. Clinical trials, peer-reviewed studies, FDA approvals... The usual documentation for health products."

Eliza is staring at me with amazement, and I realize this might be the first time anyone has pushed against her mother's whims.

"I... I'd have to get back to you on the specifics," Emma says, her confidence shaken.

"Take your time." I smile. "I never make business decisions without thorough research."

Emma forces a laugh. "You sound just like your father in his speeches."

The comment hits its intended mark, but not in the way she expects. Instead of feeling insulted, I feel a surge of protectiveness for Eliza, who's been dealing with this manipulation her entire life.

"Actually, my father and I disagree on most things," I say. "Including what constitutes sound business practices."

Emma stares at me for a moment, recalibrating. "Well. I should make some phone calls about those... documents you requested." She gathers her materials with slightly less confidence. "Excuse me."

She disappears upstairs, leaving Eliza and me alone in the suddenly quiet living room.

"Jesus," Eliza breathes. "That was..."

"Familiar?"

She nods, sinking onto the couch. "She's been here since this morning, taking over everything."

I sit beside her, noting the tension in her shoulders. "You looked the way I feel when my father talks."

"Helpless?"

"Smaller than I actually am."

Eliza meets my eyes. "Yeah. Exactly that."

I reach for her hands, which are cold despite the warm house. "We're both bigger than our parents, you know. We don't have to shrink just because they expect us to."

"Easy to say. Harder to remember when they're right there, pushing all the buttons they installed."

"Then we remind each other." I squeeze her hands. "That's what partners do, right?"

Something in her expression shifts, softens. "Partners?"

"Yeah, remember? Working toward love... everything we said the other night?" I glance up the stairs and, seeing nobody, squeeze Eliza's thigh. "I know this is all new and complicated, but..." I take a breath. "I want to be on your team, Eliza. Whatever that looks like."

Before she can respond, I remember the thermoses I left by the door. "I brought apology cocoa. As promised."

Her smile is the first genuine one I've seen since I arrived. "You did?"

I retrieve the thermoses and hand her one, watching as she takes a careful sip. A small dot of whipped cream clings to her upper lip, and I brush it away with my thumb.

"Better?" I ask.

"Much better."

I lean in to kiss her, soft and brief, tasting chocolate and relief on her lips.

"I don't see any mistletoe," she says when we part.

"Don't need it."

She grins, and for a moment we're just us again—not

the children of difficult parents, not business owners facing uncertain futures, just two people who've found something good together.

"I have news," I say. "Good news, I think."

"Please tell me it involves your trees and not my mother."

"Definitely trees. I got an email from an investor who wants to meet at the Yule Gala. It's not guaranteed, but it's hope."

"That's amazing."

"It is… but it's also terrifying." I run a hand through my hair. "This is my last shot. If it doesn't work out…"

"Then you figure out plan C."

"We're probably up to plan F at this point."

Eliza looks at me seriously, then seems to make some kind of decision. "You could set up shop here."

"What?"

"I've got that old shed, plus a couple of other buildings. You could convert one into a greenhouse, grow your trees alongside my goats." The words come out in a rush, like she's afraid she'll lose courage if she slows down. "It wouldn't be fancy, but it would be spacious."

I stare at her, stunned by the generosity of the offer. "Eliza…"

"I'm serious. You and your tiny trees would be welcome here."

The image forms in my mind—my hydroponic setup on her land, surrounded by the chaos of her animals and the warmth of her presence. It's so far from what I originally envisioned for my business, and yet somehow, perfect anyway.

"Let's hope it doesn't come to that," I say, but I'm smiling.

"But if it does…" She shrugs. "You've got options."

"We'd be arguing with each other a lot if that happens." I run a finger along the seam of her jeans.

Eliza tilts her head and raises a brow. "And some other things, too." She leans toward me, and I feel my blood surge in my veins.

A soft bleating from outside draws our attention to the window, where Maleficent is pressed against the glass, watching us with unblinking goat eyes.

"She's judging us," Eliza says.

"Your animals have very strong opinions."

"Well, Chiron likes you, which means you pass the test."

"What about you? Do I pass your test?"

Eliza looks at me for a long moment, taking in my rumpled clothes and anxious expression and the fact that I showed up here despite her rain check.

"You pass," she says. "A plus."

From upstairs comes the sound of Emma's voice, sharp and demanding as she talks to someone on the phone. Eliza's expression tightens again.

"We're going to get through this," I tell her. "Both of our family situations. We'll support each other."

"Promise?"

"Promise. You'll be at my side for the gala; I'll help you handle your mother. We're a team."

"A team," she repeats, testing the word.

"Partners."

"I like that better than what my mother's trying to turn us into."

Outside, Maleficent has been joined by two other goats, all of them staring through the window watching us like we're an interesting TV show. One of them actually seems to have mistletoe clinging to its horns.

"Our audience is growing," I observe.

"They probably want dinner. Or they're planning something. Not sure how they got out of the barn, to be honest."

I stand and offer her my hand. "Come on. Let's herd your goats and pretend your mother isn't upstairs plotting to turn me into a before photo."

Eliza takes my hand, letting me pull her to her feet. "Thank you."

"For what?"

"For not running when you met her. For not taking her bullshit. For reminding me I'm bigger than I feel right now."

"Thank you for offering me sanctuary if I need it."

"Always," she says, and I choose to believe she means it.

24

ELIZA

"I'm sure it's fine," I tell Emma for the third time as we walk up Esther's front steps. "I doubt anyone will kick you out in the snow."

Emma adjusts her coat and checks her reflection in Esther's front window. "Well, it wasn't what I'd call *inclusive* when Eden got married without inviting me."

I kick snow off my shoes before reaching for the doorknob and mutter, "She got married in the backyard. It was a glorified picnic."

Mom harrumphs and starts to say something about Diamond Elite, and my stomach clenches. "No sales pitches."

"It's not a pitch; it's a conversation about opportunity." She opens the door before I can stop her. "There's a difference."

My sisters are all on Esther's sectional sofa, and Eva winces when she sees I'm here with our mother. Esther frowns and calls toward the kitchen, "We're going to need more wine."

"Esther, darling!" Emma pushes past me for an air kiss that Esther barely tolerates. "You look wonderful. Is that a new haircut?"

"No," Esther says flatly. She doesn't elaborate but swats our mother's wrist away when Emma reaches for Esther's long locks.

The usual chaos of family dinner feels different with Emma's presence—more performative, less genuine. My sisters greet her with varying degrees of politeness, but I can see the walls going up. Eva disappears into the kitchen. Eden finds urgent bee business to discuss with Eila. Only Nate seems cordial, but he can talk to everyone.

"Where's your young man?" Emma asks, settling herself at the head of the table like she lives here. "I was hoping to continue our conversation about business opportunities."

"Reed had to work," I say, grateful he declined tonight's invitation.

"Of course he does. Career men and their deals."

I bite back my first three responses and excuse myself to the kitchen, where Eila is helping Eva arrange appetizers on platters.

"How are you holding up?" Eila asks.

"Barely." I lean against the counter, suddenly exhausted. "Can I ask you something?"

"Always."

"How did you find a therapist? Like, what's the process?"

Eila's face lights up with genuine happiness. "Oh, Liza. I'm so glad you asked." She sets down the cheese knife and pulls me into a hug. "Esther and I do some family sessions together. It's been really helpful for both of us. I could ask if you could join us sometime, help you get connected with someone."

Relief floods through me. I'd been dreading having to navigate insurance and appointments and explanations on my own. "That would be amazing."

"Consider it done." Eila squeezes my shoulders. "I'm proud of you for asking."

"Don't get too excited. I might chicken out."

"You won't. If I can do it, so can you."

Esther appears in the doorway, pulling a gorgeous pan of cranberries and pecans from the oven. "What are we doing?"

"Therapy," I say. "And also, can I borrow something fancy for Friday night? Reed has this gala thing, and I need to look like I belong there."

"A gala?" Eva's eyes light up with the particular joy she gets from makeover opportunities. "Fun."

Esther smiles. "I have a velvet blazer that will look incredible on you. Very sophisticated, but still you."

"You sure? I don't want to ruin anything expensive."

"Eliza, you're my sister. Of course, I'm sure." She sets the hot pan on a trivet and studies my face. "This is serious with Reed, huh? If you're wearing dress-up clothes."

Before I can answer, Emma's voice carries from the dining room. "I just think it's important to be realistic about these types of relationships."

We all freeze, then creep closer to the doorway to listen.

"What do you mean?" That's Eden, her voice carefully neutral.

"Well, the Nicholas family isn't exactly known for their warm, inclusive nature," Emma continues. "They're old money, very traditional. The type who look down on people like us."

My stomach drops.

"Reed's not like that," Eden says firmly. "He was really nice at the cookie exchange."

"Of course he was nice, dear. He's not going to be rude to his girlfriend's family. But let's be honest... Do you really think someone from that world is going to commit to a woman who plays with goats?"

The casual cruelty of it takes my breath away. Not just the dismissal of my business, but the implication that Reed is playing with me, that I'm naïve for believing otherwise.

Esther nods and strides into the dining room. "That's enough." Her words carry a welcome authority, but Emma's not done.

"I'm just looking out for Eliza. The boy was incredibly condescending to me, throwing his education around like it made him better than everyone else. Very much his father's son."

Rage flares in my chest, hot and protective. I dart into the dining room with my hands fisted at my side.

"Reed was perfectly respectful to you," I say. "He was asking legitimate questions about your business."

Emma looks up, surprised by my tone. "Sweetie, I know you want to defend him, but—"

"But nothing." I sink into my chair, meeting her gaze directly. "You're wrong about him, and you're wrong about his family. Reed's not his father any more than I'm you."

"Eliza—"

"I have a business, even if you don't understand it," I continue, my voice growing stronger. "I have a solid relationship. Both with long-term potential. Reed supports my work, respects my independence, and treats me like an equal partner."

I see Esther smile out of the corner of my eye.

Emma's expression shifts, becoming harder. "And when his family pressures him to find someone more suitable? Someone from his own social circle?"

"Then that's his choice to make, but I'm not going to sabotage something good because I'm afraid it might end badly."

My phone buzzes with a text from Reed:

> How's family dinner going? Surviving Emma?

My phone buzzes again.

REED NICHOLAS

> No pressure, but if you need an escape hatch, I'm at the greenhouse for a few more hours.

Perfect timing. I hold up my phone. "Speaking of my partner, he's checking on me. Because that's what people do when they care." I stand, tossing my napkin on the table. "I'm going to see him."

"Eliza, you can't just leave in the middle of dinner," Emma protests.

"Watch me." I grab my coat from the back of my chair. I kiss the top of Eva's head, then turn to Emma. "We'll talk tomorrow about your plans for the rest of the week."

"But the Diamond Elite—"

"Spare me." I'm out the door before anyone can stop me, my heart pounding with adrenaline and something that feels surprisingly courageous.

In my truck, I sit for a moment outside Esther's house, processing what just happened. I defended Reed. I set a boundary with my mother. I chose my relationship over keeping the peace.

Most surprising of all, it felt good.

25
____

REED

By Thursday afternoon, I'm running on coffee and determination, surrounded by financial projections that need to be perfect for tomorrow night.

Eliza has been so supportive, giving me space to work but also stopping by multiple times a day to make sure I eat and pretend she's going to dump manure in the hydroponic tanks to make me laugh.

The stolen kisses under the grow lights are becoming my very favorite greenhouse activity.

My space has been transformed into what Vick charitably calls "beautiful chaos"—spreadsheets covering every available surface, sample trees arranged and rearranged, and enough backup presentations to confuse a NASA engineer.

In between it all, my mother calls incessantly about the contract I haven't signed with my father's company to start work at the first of the year.

"Reed, darling, your father is getting impatient," she says without greeting when I finally answer. "If they don't get your signature by Monday, they'll have to withdraw the offer."

"Mom, *I* declined the offer. I'm busy."

"Busy with what? Plants?" Her voice sharpens. "Reed, be practical. This investor meeting is a long shot at best."

"It's not a long shot. It's a pitch."

"Hope doesn't pay the bills, sweetheart."

She launches into a speech about sound business strategies, and I can't take it anymore. Not another second. I hang up and immediately power off my phone. I can't afford distractions, not when everything depends on tomorrow night going perfectly.

Voices outside interrupt my calculations. Through the window, I see Vick and Kash approaching with a cooler, ahead of what appears to be a small army of people wearing elf hats.

"Intervention time," Vick announces, pushing through the door. "You look like hell."

"Thanks for the pep talk."

"Seriously, when's the last time you consumed something that wasn't coffee?"

Before I can answer, the Storm sisters file in behind Kash, all of them dressed like elves. Eden has a thermos that smells suspiciously alcoholic. Eila carries a six-pack in each arm. Eva's got a very fancy camera slung around her ugly holiday sweater. Bringing up the rear is Eliza herself, beaming, unfazed by this incredible act of mercy.

"What is this?" I ask.

"The boyfriend treatment," Esther announces, setting down a bag that clinks with bottles. "Our sister said you're stressed, and we've got some downtime."

"Stressed is an understatement." I gesture at the

surrounding chaos, dropping a kiss on Eliza's head. "I have one shot at this, and I'm nowhere near ready."

"Good thing you've got us," Eva says, already snapping photos. "I've been looking at your website, and honestly, it's tragic. We're going to fix that."

"You don't have to—"

"Reed, shut up and let us help," Esther interrupts, pouring eggnog into mason jars. "It's spiked. Consider it liquid courage."

FOR THE REST of the night, my friends and my girlfriend's family take over my life, but not in a way that feels intrusive or infantilizing, like when my parents overstep. No, this is somehow exactly what I didn't know to ask for but desperately needed. Eva creates a digital presence for my business, posting sleek graphics and incredible images that draw about a thousand interactions online before I finish my nog.

Eila, careful to reiterate that she, too, is garbage with paperwork, shows me financial software that prints the exact reports I need at the click of a button.

"Speaking as a professional horticulturist," she says, typing rapidly, "these trees aren't just plants; they're sustainable lifestyle choices. Price them accordingly."

Meanwhile, Esther, Eden, and Vick work on packaging and presentation. They help me repot my trees in elegant containers and create gift tags that somehow give my hydroponic seedlings a premium holiday look.

"These are gorgeous," Eden says, adjusting a tiny tree

in its new home. "I can totally see people wanting these for their apartments."

"Now all you need is a hot date by your side," Esther adds as Eliza shoves her shoulder playfully.

As the evening progresses and the spiked eggnog flows, I find myself relaxing for the first time in days. It's all overwhelming—the community, the collaboration, the sense that we're all working toward something meaningful together. This feeling has been absent from my life for far too long.

My phone, which I've reluctantly turned back on, starts ringing again. My father's number.

"Answer it," Eliza says firmly. She's been quietly helping with plant photography, but now she's watching me with that fierce expression I recognize from the barn. "Tell him what you told me about choosing your own path."

"Reed, this is ridiculous," Esther says. "You're clearly passionate about this work, and you're good at it. Why would you give that up for some corporate job you don't want?"

I look around at the transformed space—at my friends and Eliza's sisters working together to support something they see I believe in, at the trees that represent months of careful research I've loved.

"You're right," I say, answering the phone.

"Finally. Son, we need to discuss this contract situation. Your mother says you're still playing with plants instead of focusing on your future."

"I *am* focusing on my future. Just not the one you planned for me."

Silence on the other end for a beat. "Reed, be reasonable. This hobby isn't a career path you can raise a family with."

"It's not a hobby. It's a business, and it's mine."

"What's your plan to survive when the money runs out?"

"Honestly, Dad, I don't know. And that's okay. I have a lot of resources."

He snorts. "A lot less if I cut you off at the purse, kid. We had a deal, you and I."

Around me, my friends and the Storm sisters have gone quiet, listening to a conversation years in the making.

"Your grandfather would be ashamed," my father says.

"Maybe. And you're right that you and Mom have given me a really strong start in this life, but it's time I used it how I want. I hope you'll be with me as I chase my own dreams."

The silence stretches so long I think he's hung up. Then, his gruff voice filters through. "We'll discuss this later."

"No, we won't. I'm declining the Nicholas Industries position. Permanently."

I hang up to cheers and applause from my impromptu support crew. Eliza immediately hands me a cup of spiked eggnog, and Vick claps me on the back hard enough to spill it.

"To Reed Nicholas," Kash announces, raising his cup, "for finally growing a backbone."

"To Urban Forest Solutions," Eliza counters, "and to taking risks for the right reasons."

We toast, and I feel lighter than I have in months.

Whatever happens tomorrow night, at least I'm facing it as myself instead of as my father's disappointing son.

My phone buzzes with an email notification. Probably my parents sending me articles about failed entrepreneurs or statistics about business failure rates.

Instead, it's from Jennifer Martinez at North Shore Capital.

> Mr. Nicholas,
>
> I sincerely apologize for the short notice, but I've come down with the flu and will not be able to attend tomorrow evening's event. Perhaps we could schedule a meeting for after the holidays?
>
> Best regards,
> Jennifer Martinez

I read the email twice, then set my phone down carefully.

"What is it?" Eliza asks, noting my expression and rubbing my arm.

"My investor. She's sick. She's not coming tomorrow."

The greenhouse goes silent except for the hum of grow lights and the distant sound of traffic. Around me, perfectly packaged trees sit ready for a presentation that no longer has an audience. This reeks of my father's intervention.

"Fuck," Vick says simply.

I sink onto a stool, staring at months of work that suddenly feels pointless. "I was never going to succeed at this."

"Hey," Eliza says sharply. "Don't you dare."

"Eliza, face facts. I have no investors, no way forward,

and parents who are going to spend the rest of my life saying, 'I told you so.'"

"You have something better than investors right now." She gestures around the greenhouse. "You have people who believe in you. You have a product that works. And you have proof that your ideas can bring people together."

I look around at the faces surrounding me—friends who gave up their Thursday night to help me succeed, sisters who barely know me but showed up because I matter to Eliza.

"One investor doesn't make or break your entire future," Eden adds. "There are other people with money who care about sustainability."

"And honestly," Eva says, still typing on her phone, "your socials are going to generate interest whether or not tomorrow night works out. I've been posting reels like crazy, and the response is already incredible."

I want to trust that they're right. This isn't the end of everything.

It's hard to imagine a life outside my parents' sphere of influence, though.

"Fuck it," Eliza says, crushing her cup with a strong hand. "We're going to a fancy-ass party tomorrow. We're going to have a ton of fun and regroup. We'll figure something out."

Kash nods. "You can always work for me if you need money for rent," he says, waving a hand around. "It's not like you don't have advanced degrees."

Vick snaps his fingers. "Yeah, dude. Go to the party. Light a Yule log on fire. No regrets."

The air feels heavy as everyone files out. Eliza tells

her family she's going to drive me home since she abstained from the nog, and I had quite a bit.

I want to trust her. If her unconventional goat business can keep the lights on, surely we can find a way forward with my mini trees.

Maybe I'll feel more hopeful in the morning. Right now, I sort of wish her herd had finished eating my entire crop.

26

ELIZA

REED SLUMPS AGAINST MY PASSENGER SEAT LIKE A BALE OF wet hay, his typical ramrod posture completely abandoned. Either the eggnog hit him hard, or he's more stressed than he admitted about his business.

"You can take the carpool lane," he mumbles, his voice thick with alcohol and disappointment.

I glance at him as I navigate the highway toward his neighborhood, taking in the way exhaustion has settled into the lines around his eyes. There's dark stubble shadowing his jaw, and his hair sticks up at odd angles where he's been running his hands through it. He looks older somehow, depleted in a way that makes my chest ache.

"It was all pointless," he says, staring out the window at the twinkling Christmas lights lining the streets. "Two years of research, and for what? So I could prove my father right about me being impractical?"

"It wasn't pointless." I turn the radio down, where Bing Crosby is crooning about white Christmases. "One investor canceling doesn't erase everything you've accomplished."

"What have I accomplished? I grew some tiny trees nobody wants to buy."

"Reed." I pull into his apartment complex parking lot and face him fully. "What about a loan? There have to be people out there who—"

"You don't understand." His eyes are glassy with more than just alcohol. "It's not just about finding funding. It's about whether any of this matters. Whether I'm just playing with expensive toys while pretending to save the world."

The vulnerability in his voice pierces my heart. I recognize that tone, that particular flavor of self-doubt that comes from having people dismiss my own ideas as naïve or insignificant.

"I understand more than you think," I whisper. "Do you know how many times I've been told that goat landscaping is a cute hobby? That I should get a real job and leave the weed work to men with chemicals?"

Reed's head lolls against the headrest as he studies my face. "That's different. Your business works."

"My business works because I believed in it even when nobody else did. Just like yours works." I brush a strand of hair from his forehead, noting how warm his skin feels. "The difference is, I've had years to develop a thick skin about the criticism. You're still learning."

He closes his eyes at my touch. "Maybe I should just take my father's job. At least then I'd be okay financially."

"Okay how? Do you need rent money?" I let my fingers trail down to cup his cheek, feeling the scratch of stubble against my palm. "Reed, look at me."

He opens his eyes, and I see the boy he must have been—eager to please, desperate for approval, terrified of being a disappointment.

"I have news," I say. "The city finally paid me. Direct deposit hit my account this morning."

His brows furrow in confusion. "That's ... that's great. You can pay your bills now."

"I can pay my bills and then some." I lean closer, watching recognition dawn in his expression. "But more importantly, it means I'm not here because I owe you anything anymore. I'm not obligated to help you or support you or care about your success."

"Eliza—"

"I'm here because I *want* to be. My whole damn family showed up tonight because they see how much you matter to me." My voice gets softer. "I want to go to that gala with you tomorrow night, Reed. Not because you're going to pitch trees to rich people, but because it'll be fancy and fun and we can play dress-up like fairy tale characters."

A slow smile spreads across his face, the first genuine one I've seen all evening. "Fairy tale characters?"

"You'll be my dapper prince, and I'll be your fierce princess. We'll eat fancy food and dance badly and laugh at people who take themselves too seriously." I trace my thumb along his cheekbone. "If anyone asks about your trees, we'll flash the fancy photos Eva put online."

"You really want to do that? Even though I'm a schlump?"

I chuckle. "When I met you, I was wearing two sports bras to cancel out the holes. I thrive among schlumps."

Reed catches my hand and presses it against his cheek. "How did I get so lucky?"

"You didn't get lucky. You got stubborn about pursuing something you believed in, and I happen to find mulish men sexy as hell."

A Christmas song comes on the radio—something soft and jazzy about snow falling—and for a moment we just sit in my truck, surrounded by the swell of brass instruments.

"I should get you inside," I say. "You need water and sleep."

"Will you come up? Make sure I don't fall down the stairs?"

I study his face, looking for signs that this is the alcohol talking, but his eyes are clearer now, more focused. "If you want me to."

"I always want you to."

His apartment building is modest but well-maintained, with garland wrapped around the stair railings and tiny white lights outlining each doorway. As we climb to the second floor, Reed's arm around my shoulders more for comfort than support, I notice a small, wrapped package hanging from his door handle.

"What's that?" I ask, pointing to the gift.

Reed blinks at it in surprise, then carefully removes the tag. "It's from Mrs. Gustavo next door. Homemade cookies." His voice gets thick again, but not from the eggnog this time.

"See?" I squeeze his waist. "You are cared for. You are loved. Mrs. Gustavo doesn't bake cookies for people she thinks are wasting their lives."

His apartment is exactly what I expected—clean,

organized, but somehow warmer than I imagined. There's a small Christmas tree on the corner table, decorated with simple white lights and ornaments I recognize from the market vendors we met. A stack of books sits on his coffee table next to a mug that says "World's Okayest Scientist."

"Did you decorate?" I ask, hanging my coat on his kitchen chair.

"A little." He sets Mrs. Gustavo's cookies on the counter and turns to face me. "Eliza, about what you said in the car…"

"What about it?"

"You really think I'm prince material?"

I step closer, noting how the soft light from his Christmas tree makes his eyes look warmer, less haunted. "You, Saint Nicholas, are something I'm not ready to lose."

Reed reaches for me then, his hands settling on my waist with the careful reverence of someone handling something precious.

My heart does something acrobatic in my chest. "I love you," I say. "I'm not going anywhere, even if your trees never make you a dime."

When he kisses me, he tastes like eggnog and hope.

27

REED

Bramblewood Manor looks, to quote my girlfriend, "festive as fuck."

Ice sculptures gleam under chandeliers, and my trees—infinitely more elegant than they did in my greenhouse—serve as centerpieces throughout the main hall. Through the tall glass doors, I can see Eliza's cleared garden strung with hundreds of tiny white lights, and beyond that, an actual ice rink where professional dancers glide in perfect synchronization.

I adjust my jacket for the hundredth time, scanning the crowd of Pittsburgh's finest in their holiday best. Everyone appears magazine-ready, coiffed to the nines, and I'm trying not to think about how I don't belong here any more than I did at my father's presentation.

Where the hell is Eliza?

She insisted on meeting me here instead of letting me pick her up—something about last-minute animal emergencies and making sure Eden and Nate were settled at her place to keep Emma from "accidentally" releasing the goats. I check my phone again; she's only ten minutes late, but it feels like an hour.

If I'm honest, meeting her here gives me some much-needed time to cool down. I called my father before I left and told him I hoped I wouldn't see him tonight at the gala. He, of course, scoffed at the suggestion he would be here. And why should he, with nothing in it for him? I made sure he heard me assert I would not be starting work at the family firm, and he was in the middle of telling me how I'd regret that when I hung up the phone.

Then I drove to this ball where I have nothing to lose, on the edge of ruin. And I'm not sorry, because I'm meeting someone here who lights me up from the inside.

Then I see her.

Eliza Storm walks through the entrance wearing a black velvet pantsuit that makes every other woman in the room look underdressed. The jacket is cut perfectly, hugging her curves, and there's something about the way the lapels frame her chest that makes my mouth go dry. Her hair, usually in a practical ponytail, falls in soft waves around her shoulders, and someone—probably Eva—has done something magical with makeup that makes her eyes look enormous.

But it's the confidence in her stride that really gets me. She moves through this crowd of society people like she owns the place, scanning the room until her gaze lands on me.

"Holy shit," I breathe, weaving through conversations and champagne glasses to reach her. "You're gorgeous."

"You clean up pretty well yourself," she says, but I can see a hint of nervousness beneath her polished frosting.

"You look..." I search for words that aren't completely

inappropriate for public consumption. "Absolutely stunning."

I take her hand and bring it to my lips, pressing a kiss to her knuckles while maintaining eye contact. "I am the luckiest man in this room."

Her smile transforms from nervous to radiant. "Smooth, Saint Nicholas."

"Come on," I say, offering her my arm. "Let me introduce you to some people as my amazing girlfriend, the urban goatherd."

"You're really going to lead with the goats?"

"I'm leading with amazing. And girlfriend."

For the next hour, I do exactly that. Every conversation, every introduction, I make sure people know Eliza runs a successful sustainable landscaping business, that she's brilliant and fearless and the reason half this room is enjoying the stunning outdoor views tonight. Of course, I emphasize she's mine. I keep an arm around her shoulders. I let my thumb caress the velvet material. I relax into my place at her side like I never intend to leave.

And I don't.

Eliza, to my continued amazement, holds her own with every single person we meet. She talks shop with environmental lawyers, explains invasive species management to city planners, and somehow makes goat husbandry sound fascinating.

"Reed! Eliza!" Mandy Warnick appears at my elbow, looking genuinely pleased to see us both. "You two look wonderful."

"Mandy," I say, surprised by her warm tone. "Thank you again for including my trees in the decorations. They look incredible."

"They're the hit of the evening. Everyone's asking about them." She gestures to a group of stern-looking men in expensive suits standing near the refreshment table. "In fact, I was just talking to some guests who might be interested."

The men approach, and Mandy makes introductions. They're urban development executives, and from their expressions, they're dealing with some kind of professional frustration.

"Gentlemen, this is Reed Nicholas of Urban Forest Solutions, and Eliza Storm of Mobile Urban Natural Clearing Herd."

One of the men—Harrison something—shakes our hands perfunctorily. "Development in the city has been a nightmare lately. We've got this condo complex finishing up, supposed to be luxury furnished units for young tech professionals, but three different decorating contracts fell through. Place looks sterile as a hospital."

"When do you need it ready?" Eliza asks.

"January first. We've got a crop of robotics interns starting then, and these kids expect Pinterest-worthy living spaces. Even the damn scientists are social media influencers these days." Harrison gestures dismissively. "Impossible timeline for anything decent."

"Do the condos need any plant life?" Eliza asks, and I catch something calculating in her tone.

Harrison laughs. "Lady, they need everything. But we're talking about forty units that need to look like this" —he waves around the elegantly decorated room—"in just over a week."

"This guy can get you situated in no time," Eliza says, hooking her thumb at me with casual confidence. She reaches into what I now notice is a tiny pocket strategically placed near her cleavage and produces a crisp new business card that definitely wasn't designed by me.

Harrison takes the card, examining it with interest. "Urban Forest Solutions. What exactly do you do?"

"Hydroponic fir trees," I say, finding my voice. "Perfect for furnished spaces—living decorations that don't require soil or complicated maintenance. Each unit could have at least one, plus I can coordinate with other local vendors for complementary decor."

"Local vendors?" Eliza furrows her brow and taps her lip.

I nod and reference some of the people I know from the market downtown. "But Eliza's sister Eva is actually a social media influencer." I pull out my phone and show off some of the posts Eva made for my business. "I'm certain the two of us could get you what you need in time." I sip the rest of my champagne, place the flute on a nearby tray, and lean against Eliza as if I were totally calm and used to this sort of interaction rather than buzzing like a clogged hydroponic pump inside my suit. "Provided, of course, you have the budget for procurement."

"Budget, he says," Harrison muses. "It's the skillset and the items causing us trouble. You can do all that around the holidays?"

I nod as Eliza slips her hand inside my pants pocket and does indecent things with her fingertips along my thigh. With a gulp, I tell Harrison, "Give me the weekend to recover from this gala, and I promise I'll make your roboticists happy."

Harrison pockets the card and selects one of my sample trees from a nearby centerpiece. "I'll call you on

Monday with specifications. This could solve a major headache."

As the development executives move away, Harrison carrying his tiny tree like a trophy, I turn to Eliza in complete amazement.

"What just happened?"

"You just landed a massive contract, I think, and got my baby sister some design work." She grins at my stunned expression. "You better dance with me to celebrate."

"I'm a terrible dancer. And my ankle's still tender."

"Could we put some ice on it? I want to twirl around this fancy room with my hot prince."

"It's not too bad." I give it a shake, focusing on how amazing she looks right now in that suit. "Maybe you can rub it for me later." I take her hand and lead her to the small area where other couples are swaying to the string quartet. As we move—me trying not to step on her feet, her laughing at my concentrating face—I find myself staring down the front of her jacket. Thinking about her fingers in my pants pocket. Noticing her lack of a shirt under this black velvet...

"Reed," she says after a few minutes.

"Hmm?"

"My eyes are up here."

Heat floods my face. "Sorry. It's just... are you wearing anything under that jacket?"

"Wouldn't you like to know?" Her voice is pure temptation.

My pants tighten. "Yes, I *absolutely* would like to know."

She leans closer, her breath warm against my ear. "Do

you want to stay here and make small talk with more strangers, or would you like to take me to your place and get a proper look?"

I nearly trip over my own feet. "That's not really a fair choice."

"I'm not feeling particularly fair tonight."

I look around the party—at the elegant decorations, the successful people networking and celebrating, the world I thought I needed to prove myself to. Then I look at Eliza, mischief dancing in her eyes, offering me something infinitely better than professional validation.

"Get your coat," I say.

"Yes, sir."

As we make our way toward the exit, I catch sight of my trees scattered throughout the room, my work finally being appreciated and valued. But for the first time since I started this business, that recognition feels secondary to the woman beside me, who just changed my entire future with cardstock pulled from her cleavage and the unshakeable belief that I was worth investing in.

28

ELIZA

"CAN YOU STAY TONIGHT?" REED ASKS AS WE CLIMB THE stairs to his apartment, his hand warm on my lower back.

"Try to make me leave, and I'll bite you," I tell him, squeezing his arm.

"What about the goats?" He fumbles with his keys adorably, flustered.

I laugh and add to his distraction by rubbing his butt. "Eden's managing both my mother and my beasties. I'm sure they'll survive one night without me."

The moment his door closes behind us, something shifts in the air between us. The playful energy from the party transforms into something hungrier, more urgent. Reed's eyes are dark as he watches me pull off his tie, the silk sliding through my fingers.

"You have no idea what you've been doing to me all night," he says, his voice rough.

"Actually, I have some idea." I work on his belt, my fingers brushing against the firm plane of his stomach. "You haven't exactly been subtle."

"Can you blame me?" His hands settle on my waist, thumbs tracing the velvet. "You've been driving me insane."

Instead of answering, I push his jacket off his shoulders and start on the buttons of his shirt. Reed groans and reaches for my jacket, peeling it open with reverent hands.

When he sees me underneath—nothing but skin and the faint lines from the velvet—his composure completely shatters.

"Jesus, Eliza."

He drops to his knees in front of me, and I brace myself against the wall as his mouth finds my collarbone, then lower. He smells different tonight—cedar and lime instead of the earthy plant scents that usually cling to him, or the hay from our first time in the barn. This is Reed in his element, clean and polished and wild with want.

For me.

His tongue circles one nipple while his hand cups the other breast, and I arch against the wall, fingers tangling in his hair. He's methodical, using the same focused attention he gives his trees. I'm already close to falling apart when I tug him up by his ears.

"Where's your bedroom?" I pant.

"Down the hall."

We practically sprint there, shedding clothes and laughing as we collide with doorframes and each other. By the time we reach his bed, I'm in nothing but the borrowed suit pants, and he's down to his boxers.

"Wait," he says as I reach for his waistband. "I should mention... I'm completely healthy. Had my physical last month, clean bill of health." He pauses, suddenly looking shy. "If you wanted to consider… intercourse."

I burst out laughing. "Intercourse? Really?"

"What would you prefer I call it?"

"Sex, Reed. Fucking. Banging." I kiss his neck, tasting salt and cedar. "And I haven't been with anyone in a few years, so you'd be my first in a while. I have a birth control implant."

His fingers find the tiny device in my arm, and he presses a kiss to the spot. "Are you saying we could have sex without a condom? Because I don't have any."

"Actually, Esther shoved a peppermint-scented condom in these pants just in case," I admit, patting my pocket. "But I'm good if you are."

Reed's eyes go wide. "Your sister gave you condoms?"

"My sister is very passionate about safe sex. But like I said, I'm good if you are."

I push him onto the bed and take a moment to really look at him. He's beautiful in the lamplight—long lines and lean muscle, dark hair trailing down his stomach to frame his cock, which is impressively hard and stands straight against his belly.

"You're gorgeous," I tell him, running my hands down his chest.

He smiles softly at those words, almost looking innocent. "I want you so much, Eliza. It's… unholy." His voice is strained. "Is there a position you like?"

I bite my lip, suddenly feeling bold. "Do you care if I'm on top?"

He moans, and his hips jut up beneath me. "I can't wait to see you on top of me."

The want in his voice sends heat straight between my legs. I'm wet from our foreplay in the living room. Honestly, I was wet the moment he said hello to me in that suit. I straddle his hips, positioning myself over his length, and slowly sink onto him as Reed stares in wide-eyed wonder.

The sensation is overwhelming—fullness and stretch and perfect friction that makes my bones feel like they're melting. Reed's hands grip my hips, his head thrown against the pillows as I adjust to the feeling of him inside me.

"Move," he breathes. "Please, Eliza. Move."

I start with small rocking motions, finding my rhythm, watching his face as pleasure transforms his features. When I find the angle that makes stars explode behind my eyelids, I ride him harder, chasing that bright edge of sensation.

"That's it," Reed gasps. "You look so fucking beautiful like this."

His thumb finds my clit, and the combination of his touch and the feeling of him moving inside me sends me over the edge. I come with a cry that echoes off his bedroom walls, my body clenching around him.

"My turn," he growls, flipping us over before I've finished shaking. He hooks my legs over his wrists, spreading me wide, and the new angle makes me gasp.

"This is very un-saint-like, Mr. Nicholas," I manage to say, and he grins.

"Are you complaining?"

"Hell no. I'm here for it."

He sets a rhythm that has me building toward another peak, his movements steady and sure. I love him like this—savage and unhinged, completely overcome with desire. And it's for me. For us.

I watch his body stiffen as he gets closer to his own orgasm, and I lick my lips, swept up in the image of him this way, knowing I'm the only one who will ever get to see this. When he comes, it's with a roar I feel in my chest, his body shuddering as he spills inside me.

AFTERWARD, we lie tangled together, both of us breathing hard. Reed kisses my shoulder, my neck, any part of me he can reach.

"I have something to tell you," he says against my collarbone.

"If it's about your stamina, I'm impressed."

He laughs. "No, but thank you. It's about tonight. What you did at the party."

"What about it?"

"I was only *falling* in love with you before," he says quietly. "But watching you work that room and pull a trick from your actual bosom... I know it now. I love you, Eliza. I love your goats and your ridiculous donkey and your ramshackle property with the best views in Pittsburgh."

My heart does something complicated in my chest. "Reed..."

"I love your family and your tenacity and the way you see possibilities I miss completely." He lifts his head to look at me. "I want to spend every Yule with you. Every holiday, every season. I want to build something together that's bigger than either of us could manage alone."

I cup his face, noting the stubble that's grown rougher since this morning, the way his eyes look soft and vulnerable in the lamplight.

"I love you, too," I tell him. "All of you. Even when you overthink and use words like 'intercourse.'"

"Especially those parts?"

"Especially those parts."

He kisses me then, slow and thorough, tasting like champagne and promises. Outside, snow is falling past his windows, and somewhere in the city, my goats are probably plotting their next escape. But here, wrapped around Reed in his warm bed, everything feels exactly as it should be.

"So," I say when we break apart. "What's the plan for tomorrow?"

"Sexual intercourse. Make you breakfast. Call Eva about our new project..."

"Sounds perfect."

"You realize this means you're stuck with me now, right? Business partner, personal partner, everything."

I grin. "Promise?"

"You're not getting rid of me, Storm."

"Good," I say, pulling him in for another kiss.

EPILOGUE: ELIZA
ONE YEAR LATER

THE SCENT OF WOOD SMOKE AND PEPPERMINT FILL MY farmhouse as I pad through rooms that look absolutely different from a year ago, but feel ten times more comfortable. Where once I had mismatched everything and tools scattered haphazardly, Reed's organizational systems now complement my chaotic energy in ways that somehow make perfect sense.

His dark jeans hang next to my overalls in the mudroom. His polished dress shoes—though, he rarely needs them anymore—sit beside my work boots on a proper shoe rack by the door. In the kitchen, his French press shares counter space with my ancient coffee maker, because apparently, we both need caffeine in different formats to function.

The real magic happened outside, though. Reed converted the old shed into his hydroponic headquarters, complete with climate control that makes my animals jealous during Pittsburgh's bitter winters. The smaller outbuilding became his specialty operation—hydroponic mistletoe that's already pre-sold with a wait list. Turns out, rich people will pay ridiculous money for locally grown toxic parasites with a romantic backstory.

"You're supposed to be getting dressed," Reed murmurs against my neck, his arms sliding around my waist as I stand daydreaming at the kitchen window in my striped pajamas, watching snow dust the goat pen.

"So are you," I point out, leaning against his chest. He's wearing matching pajamas—red and white candy cane stripes that Eva insisted we needed for hosting duties. "But you're the one who started this by making those peppermint mochas that smell wintery and magical."

A laugh rumbles through his chest. "I distinctly remember you being the one who suggested we 'warm up' by the fire before people arrived." After our very acrobatic session in the living room, where we narrowly avoided burning his butt cheeks on the stove, I'm a bit sore and a lot relaxed.

I turn in his arms, studying his face in the golden light. A year of living together has softened some of his sharper edges. He's more likely to laugh now, less likely to overthink every decision into paralysis. The daily physical work of farm life has broadened his shoulders and roughened his hands in ways that make my stomach flutter. And we help each other with paperwork, so neither of us gets as stressed about it.

Personally, I think the hottest change was when we worked together to set up boundaries with our shitty parents. Once Emma realized nobody in our family was buying into her predatory pyramid scheme, she split town. We have a Storm pact not to let her cross our thresholds unless she calls ahead and we *all* feel ready to see her. Reed, meanwhile, has been cut off financially, and that's seemed more like a favor than a punishment. He sees his mom when he feels up to it, on his terms, and hasn't pulled out his formal attire since the Yule gala last year.

"No regrets about this?" I ask, gesturing around our kitchen, where his calibrated measuring cups coexist with my "pinch of this, splash of that" cooking style.

"About living with a woman whose donkey broke my ankle and whose goats ate my life's work?" Reed grins and pulls me closer. "Not a single one."

"Even when therapy is kicking both our asses?"

"Especially then." His expression grows more serious. "Marsha says the exhaustion means it's working."

He's right. The joint sessions with our therapist have been brutal some weeks—pulling apart old patterns, learning to fight fair, figuring out how to be a team instead of two people trying to manage everything alone. But Reed beside me in those uncomfortable chairs makes even the worst sessions bearable.

"Speaking of hard work paying off," I say, tracing the edge of his pajama collar, "Harrison called yesterday. He wants to book you for three more condo complexes."

Reed's face lights up. "Seriously?"

"Seriously. Apparently, photos of your trees in those tech worker apartments went viral on LinkedIn, and now everyone wants Urban Forest Solutions to stage their corporate housing." I grin at his shocked expression. "Plus, Eva's booked solid through spring doing the styling work. My baby sister is making more money than any of us."

"Speaking of Eva," Reed says, glancing toward the front window where headlights are starting to appear in our driveway, "she seemed weird when she stopped by yesterday. Distracted."

"She got some official-looking mail she's pretending doesn't exist. Certified delivery and everything." I shrug. "She says she doesn't want to deal with new business until after the holidays, but you know Eva. She's probably just nervous about meeting your engineering friends."

Reed snorts. "Paolo, Vick, and Kash should be the ones who are nervous. Eva's going to destroy them in the gingerbread competition."

Car doors slam outside, followed by the unmistakable sound of my sisters arguing about something. Through the window, I can see them all climbing out of Esther's car, every single one of them wearing matching striped pajamas. Even Koa has somehow been convinced to participate, his massive frame covered in candy cane stripes and topped with an elf hat that makes him look like a very large, very serious ornament.

"Man," Reed breathes, watching the Storm parade approach our front door. "Your family is something else."

"*Our* family," I correct, because my sisters have adopted Reed completely. "And they're about to invade our cozy morning."

Before I can finish the thought, the front door bursts open without anyone bothering to knock—the way I prefer them to enter our home. Ben appears first, carrying enough gingerbread supplies to construct a small village, followed by Eden and Nate hauling coolers that undoubtedly contain Eila's latest beer experiments.

"We brought reinforcements!" Paolo's voice carries from behind them as Reed's friends file in, all of them also wearing matching pajamas. Vick has on red stripes, Kash chose green, and Paolo went with blue. They look like a very nerdy boy band. Or an international *Where's Waldo* conference.

"Oh good," Eva says, eyeing Reed's friends with the calculating expression she gets when she's planning online content. "The engineers are here. I was hoping for a real challenge this year."

"Challenge accepted," Vick says solemnly, which makes Eila snort with laughter.

"Should we be concerned that Eva looks terrifying?" Reed murmurs in my ear as our house fills with the familiar chaos of Storm family gatherings.

"Probably. A few years ago, she built a gingerbread replica of Three Rivers Stadium. Complete with working lights."

"Dang." He rubs his scruff against my cheek, reminding me how it felt against my thighs an hour earlier.

Before I lose my composure entirely, Esther appears at my elbow with a coffee mug shaped like a tiny Christmas tree—one of Reed's prototypes that she commandeered months ago. "You two need a timeout or a cold shower," she teases. "I can feel the burning hot Yule energy between you."

"We're hosting," I protest. "We should be comfortable."

"You're distracting the men," she says, nodding

toward where Reed's friends are trying very hard not to stare at Reed's hand on my candy cane-striped ass. "Nate hasn't blinked in five minutes."

Before I can argue, a tremendous bray erupts from outside, followed by the distinctive sound of Chiron's hooves against the kitchen window. Through the glass, his enormous gray head appears, ears pinned in what might be annoyance or excitement—it's hard to tell with donkeys.

"Should we invite him in?" I ask Reed, only half-joking. "He's clearly feeling left out."

"Absolutely not. Your donkey has strong opinions about my friends, and I don't need him expressing them in our living room."

Chiron brays again, louder this time, and I watch Reed's expression shift from amused to resigned. A year of living with my animals has taught him that resistance is usually futile.

"Oh, hush," he says to his four-legged friend, pressing a kiss to my cheek that tastes like peppermint and promises. "I'm going outside to put him back."

I laugh and cup his face. "I love you," I tell him, because it still feels miraculous to say it without panic.

"I love you, too," he says, then grins with the competitive gleam I recognize from his hydroponic research days. "I'll be back in time to kick some Storm butt with my gingerbread igloo."

Outside, Chiron brays his approval, and inside, our house fills with laughter and the promise of another perfectly chaotic storm.

🌲

Curious about Eva's certified mail? Grab her book Sappy
Go Lucky to learn what's going on.

Looking for more Eliza and Reed? My newsletter
subscribers get a steamy bonus scene. Visit
LaineyDavis.com to subscribe or scan the QR code
below!

OTHER STORM SISTERS BOOKS

Bridges and Bitters series

Fireball: An Enemies to Lovers Romance (Sam and AJ)

Liquid Courage: A Marriage in Crisis Romance (Chloe and Teddy)

Speed Rail: A Single Dad Romance (Piper and Cash)

Last Call: A Marriage of Convenience Romance (Esther and Koa)

Planted and Plowed series

Against the Grain (Eila and Ben)

The Burgh and the Bees (Eden and Nate)

Yule Be Sorry (Eliza and Reed)

Sappy Go Lucky (Eva and Asher)

Since You've Bean Gone (Ethan and Lia) *part of the Farm 2 Forking series